RUIN

on the River

AN ALEX PAIGE MYSTERY

THERESA L CARTER

Contents

Chapter 1

Alex pressed on the accelerator, her speed increasing rapidly as she pulled out of the curve only to slow down again for the next one. She headed straight for a canopy. Under it, a photographer pointed a long lens at her, panning as she followed the contours of the barely-two lane road and passed within inches of the man. A large banner advertised a website where drivers could find pictures of themselves conquering the Tail of the Dragon. The scenic drive snaked around 318 turns over a mere eleven miles, making the mountain passage from Tennessee to North Carolina the curviest in the United States.

"Now that's entrepreneurial," Emily said.

"Smart," Alex agreed. She risked a glance at her friend, who was grinning as she held onto the bar above her window, her fuchsia mohawk brushing the glass of the moon roof. "How much do you think they charge for the photos?"

"I'm sure we'll find out," Emily said. "Makes sense someone would do this. It's like the photo ops at amusement parks, and this is kind of like a roller coaster."

"I wonder how they get permission to sit there?" Alex mused.

"Always the reporter," Emily chuckled.

Alex smiled. Emily was right. Alex may have retired from reporting to become a travel writer, but her journalistic instincts were as sharp as ever. During her newspaper days, she'd focused on crime and corruption cases, but after digging into one too many stories of people trying to get away with murder–sometimes literally–she couldn't take it anymore. She turned in her notice, boarded a plane for Arizona for her first travel story, and never looked back. As she hugged the shoulder around another curve, she thought of her friend William. She'd met the fellow writer during one of her first press trips. They'd instantly hit it off, even though they'd both had a crush on the same guy. "Glad you don't mind being a passenger," she said to Emily, coming back to the present. "William would have insisted on driving."

"I can't believe a man who specializes in road trips gets carsick."

"Only if he's not driving." Alex eased back in her seat as they hit a straight stretch for a few yards. They were on their way to Asheville and had decided to skip I-40 and take a detour along this more scenic route. They'd picked a perfect day for it. Blue skies filled the moon roof. Not that Alex could look up to see them. Occasionally she'd glimpse the smooth mountain tops and deep valleys of the Smokies, but she had to focus on the road. One downside of driving a route like this was that she couldn't soak in the views, but she was OK with that. She neared another turn, tightening her grip on the steering wheel and leaning into the curve. "Should we take this on the way home so you can drive it?"

Emily shook her head, a motion Alex barely caught in her peripheral vision. "Nah. It's lovely, but I'll have to get back to Chicago quickly. In fact, I'll probably fly back so you don't have to rush. I know you like to stick around and explore."

"This is true." Alex embraced one last curve before entering a town roaring with Harleys and sports cars. "Town" was generous:

the intersection comprised a barbecue joint, a lodge, and a gift shop where drivers could purchase the photos of their vehicles taken by the enterprising photographers, as well as every souvenir imaginable. The place was crawling. Alex lucked into a parking spot in the full lot as a '63 'Vette pulled out of a space. They stepped out of her Outback and stretched.

"That was fun," Alex said, grinning and shaking her hands loose. She inhaled the smoky scent of roasting meat combined with the exhaust of hundreds of motorcycles.

"Glad we drove this on a Friday," Emily said. "Can you imagine what it'll be like tomorrow?"

"Bumper to bumper." A man dressed in leather chaps, leather vest, leather gloves, and wearing a pink handkerchief on his head held the door to the souvenir shop open for the two women. "First time?" he asked, his voice rumbling almost as deep as one of the motorcycles. When they nodded, he smiled, revealing perfectly straight teeth and an adorable dimple.

"What gave it away?" Emily asked.

"Those shit-eating grins. What brings you to these parts?" When Alex raised an eyebrow in question, he indicated her Subaru. "Illinois plates."

"Beer," she explained.

"I'm pretty sure they've got beer where you come from," he said, following them inside.

"We're here for the Raise the Beer Fest," Emily said. "She's a travel writer and I'm just along for the ride."

"And Sergio," Alex winked at Emily.

"Y'all know Sergio? Well, Hell's bells. You must be good people." The man peeled back his glove and looked at his watch. "Darn.

I gotta get back on the road, but I'll look for you tomorrow. I'm Roger," he said, extending his hand.

Alex shook it. He headed back outside and she stared after him. "Did you see that watch?"

"Uh huh. Probably cost more than his ride."

The friends browsed the shop. Alex spun a display laden with postcards and bumper stickers. They found several photos of Alex's car on a wall of televisions, but skipped buying any once they saw how much they cost. "Yowza. Amusement park schtick. Amusement park prices," Emily said as they walked towards the exit.

Alex was not empty-handed, however. She stopped at the cashier and put a journal on the counter. The cover was a moody image of a winding river flanked by mountains shrouded in trees and mist. She shrugged when Emily shook her head at her purchase. "Some people buy shot glasses; I buy journals."

"I know," Emily said. "I've seen your shelves."

As they walked to the car, Alex checked her phone. "We've got a couple hours of driving before we get to Asheville, but we're early. There's a brewery I want to check out; mind if we stop there before heading to Layers? It's kind of on the way."

Emily sighed. "You're going to make me wait, aren't you?"

Alex paused while another cavalcade of motorcycles passed, then pulled out onto the two-lane road. "Not for long. But I've been hearing a lot about this place and I doubt we'll have time to visit before the fest tomorrow."

"Fine, but you're buying."

"Deal."

The building consumed what would have been an entire city block if it hadn't been in an industrial corridor. Monolith Brewing Company loomed in giant letters over the top of the cinder block exterior, perched above silver tanks the size of barn silos. There were no windows except for a narrow one next to the door. Two rows of picnic tables sat on the bare asphalt, bordered by raised beds filled with wilted geraniums. Above, strings of Edison lights hinted there might be a touch of ambiance once the sun set.

"So, why are we here?" Emily asked.

"I'm working on a piece about the local brewery scene. Since this place has been getting a lot of ink, even back in Chicago, I thought I should check it out."

Emily frowned. "Not a whole lot of character. Maybe the inside's better."

They entered a narrow hallway and stopped, blinking to adjust to the dim lighting. The corridor led to a cavernous warehouse space. At one end, a glass wall provided a view of the brewery operations, which could be seen from any of the high tops scattered around the room. Stacks of barrels lined the back. They walked to the bar and sat on stools, gasping as their bare thighs hit the cool metal.

"What exactly have you heard about this place?" Emily asked. "Can't imagine anyone praising the décor."

Alex looked around. She wasn't totally surprised because she'd checked out Monolith Brewing's social media accounts and websites, but she was still disappointed in how stark and utilitarian it appeared. "Not exactly the most hospitable place," she said.

Two men stood at the end of the bar. One of them, a stout man with a comb-over, looked up and frowned when he saw the two women. Alex heard him tell the other man to stock the cooler, "and do it right this time," and then he walked towards them. *More like waddled*, Alex thought, then reprimanded herself for being unkind. "Let me guess," he said, looking at Alex. "You want a wine slushie, and you," he pointed at Emily, "want a cider. Something sweet."

She and Emily turned to each other and burst out laughing. Alex decided that thinking the man waddled was just fine. "Um, no. Not even close," Emily sneered.

The man scowled. "So you're actually beer drinkers?"

Emily looked around. "We are in a brewery."

"Absolutely," Alex said brightly, giving her friend a warning glance. "I'm a travel writer doing a story about Asheville breweries."

The man's demeanor abruptly switched. He smiled, an affectation Alex thought he probably intended to be charming but creeped her out instead. "Welcome to Monolith Brewing. I'm Greg Mitchell, and I own this place." If he'd been wearing suspenders, he would have pulled them out and rocked on his heels. He turned and filled a couple of short glasses from the tap right behind him. Froth spilled over the rim. "Try that, then."

Alex took her first sip. "Tasty," she said. "Very clean."

"It's the water," Mitchell drawled. "Pure, clear, mountain water. If I could bottle that up and sell it, I would."

"You kind of are," Emily said. She eyed her glass. "You know, this reminds me of another beer. What was it," she turned to Alex. "Do you know which one I'm thinking of?"

Alex considered, then took another drink. "You're right. This tastes just like the pilsner from Zen." It was a beer they could get back in Chicago and Emily served it at Elements, her Lincoln Park restaurant.

Mitchell slapped his hand on the bar. "Our beer tastes *nothing* like that swill. Nothing." He turned to the taps and pulled a couple more short pours, sloshing beer over the rims. "Here. Try this and tell me it tastes like someone else's."

Alex and Emily glanced at each other, then accepted the glasses filled with a dark, almost black liquid with creamy foam on top. Emily grabbed a bev nap to wipe off the glass, then took a drink and coughed. "You're right about that; I've never tasted anything like it."

Mitchell beamed. The glint in his eyes spoke of a deep-seated need to win. "That right there is going to be the hit of the Raise the Beer Fest. Just you watch." He wiped down the bar and handed the towel to the bartender. "Get these ladies anything they want." The bartender nodded and Mitchell walked off.

Alex turned her chin to her shoulder and spoke under her breath. "What the heck is this?"

Emily coughed. "It tastes like Christmas and Halloween got into a fight and we lost."

"Exactly. I'm getting clove, pumpkin, cinnamon, and what's that other flavor?"

"That would be 'pine'," the bartender said, with air quotes. When they looked at him, he shrugged. "Bartender ears. I can hear conversations from across the room, let alone right in front of me."

"OK. Honest opinion. What do you think of this?" Alex asked, pointing at her glass.

He leaned over and whispered. "It's crap."

Emily laughed. "Yes, yes it is. Here," she said, shoving their glasses across the bar, "dump these and pour something you would drink."

"Before you do, what's your name?" Alex asked.

"Todd. And you?"

"Alex and Emily." Alex watched Todd turn to face the taps and walk all the way to the end, where he pulled a handle that differed from the rest. Inside the glasses he set in front of them, the liquid was opaque and nearly orange. Alex tasted it. "Oh wow. That is delicious."

Emily nodded. "So much grapefruit, but not too much, you know?"

Alex lifted her pint and pointed her index finger at the tap on the end. "This is a guest beer, isn't it?"

"Sure is. I wouldn't drink the beers made here if you paid me, and since I am actually paid to be here, that should tell you something."

"What about that one?" Alex asked, pointing to the tap of the first beer Mitchell had poured them.

Todd frowned. "Not even that one."

"But it's really good," Emily said. "It tasted just like Zen's Pils."

It was a few beats before he responded. "Exactly."

"Ahhh," Alex and Emily said simultaneously. "Do they know?" Alex asked.

"Of course. Doesn't mean they can do anything about it."

"I have to ask," Emily said, leaning forward. "If you hate this place so much, why do you work here?" Her directness was one of the many things Alex loved about her friend. "Let me guess. Is it a 'keep your enemies closer' type of thing?"

Todd winked. "I could tell you, but then I'd have to..."

"Got it."

The bartender grabbed the glasses still full of the dark liquid and dumped them in the sink behind the bar. "Are you going to the fest tomorrow?"

They nodded and Alex spoke. "That's why we're here."

"Will you be there?" Emily asked.

Todd nodded. "Yep. Pouring this crap. You won't be able to miss me. I'll be the one wearing a tarp to protect myself when people throw their cups at me." The two friends laughed. "If you're here to cover the fest, do you know about Sergio and his non-profit?"

"We sure do," Emily said, doing her best Groucho Marx impersonation.

Todd snapped his fingers. "That's right. I knew I recognized you. You were in that show; what's it called?"

"*Dining + Destinations*," Alex answered. "We met Sergio during the production and we've all stayed in touch. Some of us more than others." She winked and tipped her head toward Emily, who elbowed her.

"Cool cool." He looked up as a couple entered the bar, then turned back to Alex and Emily and pointed at their nearly empty beers. "Those two are on Mitchell. If you're looking for some real beer, head to Titan. Or you could just go to Layers since you, ahem, know the owner." He winked again at Emily, then sauntered to the end of the bar to help the arrivals.

Alex stood up, peeling her bare legs off the metal seat. She and Emily each left a few dollars on the bar and waved at Todd on the way out. He acknowledged them with a nod.

"That was interesting," Emily said after they'd climbed into Alex's Outback.

"You know what I'm realizing?" Alex asked. "That there's drama everywhere. Nothing is simple. Nothing is what it seems. There are always—"

"Layers?" Emily finished.

"Like an onion." The friends laughed.

"Speaking of layers, when is Mr. William meeting us?"

"Not until tomorrow. He and Billy got in this morning and picked up some steaks from a local butcher. They're both looking forward to 'living like mountain men,' as William put it."

Emily guffawed. "If William weren't the mountain man I know him to be, that would be hilarious."

"A mountain man with a twenty-minute facial routine and an inordinate need for beauty rest."

"He's an enigma, that one." They were silent as Alex negotiated some tight curves. "So, Layers?" Emily asked.

Alex quickly gave her friend a side glance, then smiled as she focused on the road. "Of course. I think I've made you wait long enough."

Chapter 2

The car was still rolling when Emily jumped out. She ran across the gravel and leaped, wrapping her legs around Sergio. He spun her round and round, her laughter carrying to Alex as she stepped onto the lot. She turned away as Emily's fuchsia-topped head dipped and the two exchanged a long-awaited kiss. *Ah, young love*, she thought. Alex heard rocks pinging metal behind her and turned to see a campervan pull up. The driver's window rolled down. "Alright you two, get a room," William called.

Emily turned, still wrapped around Sergio, who'd laced his fingers together underneath her to hold her up. "You don't have to tell me twice." She swung her legs down and stood, grabbing Sergio's hand and pulling him towards the row of cabins.

Sergio stayed put. Emily turned and grasped his wrist with both her hands. She pulled, feigning resistance from him as he shook his head. They were like a couple of teenagers, Alex thought. Sergio bent his head down to Emily and Alex heard him say, "Later," in a low growl. *I wonder what that's like?* It had been so long since she'd had any real physical connection with a man she'd forgotten what it felt like.

As Alex neared the couple, Emily let go, a grin plastered on her face. Sergio hugged Alex, one of those deep, connecting hugs that belied his normally gruff demeanor. She heard William and Billy approaching and released Sergio, who then turned to hug the two men. He'd barely released them when Emily barreled in, kissing both William and Billy on either cheek. "What are you two doing here? Alex said we wouldn't see you until tomorrow."

"I decided I couldn't withhold the pleasure of our presence from you any longer," William said.

"And he burned the steaks, so we're hungry," Billy said.

William gently nudged his partner, pushing his shoulder so the other man stumbled. "*We* burned the steaks, you mean. I asked you to keep an eye on them, remember?"

"I was too busy keeping an eye on something else." Billy wiggled his eyebrows, which were thick and black and slightly resembled a pair of caterpillars. They made his blue eyes even brighter.

The group of friends laughed. Alex looked at the two couples. She'd been there when each of them had met. William had fallen for Billy while the detective was investigating a murder during a Door County, Wisconsin, press trip the two writers had attended, and Sergio and Emily met while filming the pilot episode of *Dining + Destinations*, a travel cooking show. Both pairs initially seemed unlikely. William was gregarious and completely comfortable in his skin. Billy, a no-nonsense police officer, hid his orientation and seemed determined to keep it that way, but William broke through his reservations.

Sergio and Emily each had passionate temperaments, but the two chefs were uniquely suited for each other, especially since they lived several states apart.

Alex focused on the large cabin behind Sergio. It looked like it had once been a mess hall, but to the side of the log building, she could see tall tanks. She knew the Civilian Conservation Corps had built the original encampment in the 1930s as they were constructing the Blue Ridge Parkway.

Sergio caught her appraisal. "Do you want to see our little operation first, or would you like to get settled into your cabin?"

"Cabin," Alex and Emily said simultaneously.

William looked between Emily and Alex, frowning. "Alright, you two. Don't keep us waiting. You," he said, pointing at Alex. "I know how you like to get comfortable. And you," he shifted to Emily. "Don't get all distracted by Mr. Tour Guide here."

"He's just grumpy because he's hungry. I'll get him some onion rings and a beer and he'll be fine," Billy said, then walked towards the brewery.

William shrugged before following. "He gets me."

Sergio shook his head and turned to Alex. "The cabins are right over there. I can grab a couple guys to help you with your bags so you can leave your car here for now."

"No need," Emily said as she opened the gate at the back of the SUV. She pulled out a large hot pink backpack and shrugged it on, then pulled out Alex's rolling suitcase and smaller black backpack. Alex grabbed her two bags from Emily and they followed Sergio towards a curved row of log cabins sheltered by evergreens and deciduous trees about a hundred yards from the main building. As they neared, she heard water cascading over rocks. Rivers, lakes, oceans—anything related to water was like catnip to Alex and she practically ran, picking up her suitcase so the wheels wouldn't get damaged on the gravel.

She reached a creek that flowed behind the cabins, which were cleverly arranged so each back deck was hidden from the next, providing privacy. From the outside, the cabins looked exactly like they should. The weathered logs alternated with cream strips of chinking. Patches of moss on the roofs hinted at their age. The front porch extended the width of the cabin and was big enough to fit a swinging bench. "Oh, Sergio," she sighed. "This is absolutely perfect."

"Wait 'til you see the inside," he grinned, pulling out a large brass key as he approached the cabin on the end. "This one's yours. They're all private, but I know you're an early riser. This way you can have your coffee in your robe and don't have to worry about anybody seeing you." He opened the door with a flourish and Alex entered, then stopped. She stepped back out, then entered the cabin again. She poked her head back through the door. "Em, come here. You've got to see this."

Emily followed her in and they scanned the interior. It was a model of tiny home efficiency. A wood-burning fireplace with a massive stone surround acted as the centerpiece of the wall to her left. It was flanked by shelves filled with books focused on the outdoors and the Appalachians. While the designers had kept the rough-hewn logs exposed, the cabin had all the modern conveniences, except for a television. Outlets studded the walls every few feet. In the far corner, a kitchen with granite countertops and stainless steel appliances meant Alex could cook if she wanted to. The L-shaped counter provided a breakfast bar that would be a perfect spot for her morning journaling. On the window sill above the sink, herbs reached towards the sun.

"This is perfect, simply perfect. I'll get unpacked while you show Emily her cabin," she said. "See you in fifteen?"

"Make it twenty," Emily said, giving Sergio a wicked grin.

Alex unpacked, stowing her clothes in the drawers at the bottom of the bookshelves and her toiletries under the sink in the bathroom. She knew she'd be there at least a week, and while she loved to travel, she did not love living out of a suitcase. Plus, she felt making a place feel like home gave her a better sense of its character.

After placing her candle and journal on the breakfast bar, she turned off the lights and left the cabin. She figured if she waited for Emily and Sergio, she might be there all night.

She locked up and walked the path towards the building that contained Layers Brewing. A wide expanse of grass behind the brewery backed up to the creek. She could see picnic tables, chairs, and firepits strewn around the open field. Most of them were occupied, and several dogs lolled in the grass next to their people. A three-legged cat with black and gray stripes hopped onto one of the picnic tables. The man sitting at it reached over to pet it, and it flopped over on its side. Alex stopped to smile at the bucolic scene, then entered the building.

"There she is!" William shouted from the bar, drawing the attention of the few people dispersed around the space. William leaned over to look past her. "I see we've already lost the happy couple," he said.

"We're right here," Emily called from behind her, a huge grin plastered on her face. She let go of Sergio's hand and looped her arm through Alex's.

Sergio split off and walked behind the bar, approaching a woman whose skin shone like marble. She smiled, a flashing brilliance that transformed her from an impossible sculpture to a living, breathing work of art. Alex didn't think she'd ever seen anyone so beautiful. William waved his hand in front of her face. "Close your mouth, my dear, and stop staring. This here's Calliope."

The bartender wiped her hands with a towel and extended one across the bar. "Pleasure to meet you," she said.

Alex rattled her head and snapped back to reality, reaching out to shake Calliope's hand. "I'm Alex."

Emily also reached across to shake her hand. "Please forgive my friend. She's normally much more articulate."

Sergio tilted his head towards his bartender. "She's used to it."

"If I had a dime for every time someone asked me why I was bartending instead of modeling, I could buy him out," Calliope shrugged. "It's genetics. I prefer to use my skills."

"And skilled she is. She's going to be one of the best brewers out there."

"Because of you."

"I present the tools. What people do with them is up to them. Here," Sergio said, pouring tasters and passing them across the bar. They each took a drink, set their glasses on the bar, and stared at Calliope.

"Wow," they said, simultaneously.

Calliope grinned. "Glad you like it. That's our signature beer for the fest tomorrow."

"What's that flavor? I can't nail it down," Alex asked.

William leaned forward. "We've been trying to figure it out, but she won't tell us."

Calliope winked. "Find me tomorrow and I'll tell you my secret."

Alex drained her glass, then asked for a pint. "This is so much better than what we had at Monolith."

Sergio's face darkened. "You went *there*?" he scowled.

Alex raised her hands in surrender. "Work, Sergio. It's for work. I take it you don't like them?"

Calliope abruptly walked away. Sergio's eyes followed her, then turned back to his friends lining the bar, looking at them one by one. "No. I do not."

"What's the skinny? What'd we miss?" William asked, leaning forward.

Sergio shook his head. "Nothing special. Although, you'll see him tomorrow."

"Quick question," Emily said. "This fest isn't a contest, is it? I thought you didn't want to make it competitive."

"No, it isn't. We'll have a people's choice award, but that's it. This is simply to celebrate great beer—well, most of it will be great—and raise money for more scholarships."

William inhaled as if to speak, but it turned into an appreciative whistle as the front door slammed open and a tall man strode into the building, long black hair trailing behind him. "Now that is a tall drink of water."

"You know I'm right here," Billy admonished him, but then grinned. "And yes, yes he is."

The man headed straight to the bar. He raised his right hand, which was gripped tightly around something. "It's getting worse, Sergio. We have to do something about him, *now*," the man growled.

Chapter 3

"You've been to see Mitchell." Sergio stated bluntly.

The man shook his head. "I didn't see him, no. I just went to the river." He opened his fist to reveal a test tube filled with cloudy water. "I took this sample a few hours ago. The E. coli is off the charts. Sergio, we *have* to do something about him. He's killing the river and anyone who drinks his crap."

Alex and Emily stared at each other, then at Sergio. "Mitchell, as in Greg Mitchell? As in Monolith?" Alex asked.

The man turned to them. "Yes. Why? Don't tell me you're a fan."

Alex raised her hands again. "Whoa. We just met him, and from what we saw, we don't like him, and definitely don't like his beer."

He relaxed slightly, lowering his shoulders. "Sorry. It's just, that man is pure evil. He's killing the French Broad."

"Who's the French broad?" William asked. "And are we in the middle of *another* murder?" He slapped his knee, guffawing. "I crack myself up." Everyone glared at him, and he bowed his head in apology. "Right. Not a laughing matter. Got it. My apologies."

The man continued to stare, then relented as William repeated his apology. He turned back to Sergio. "We need to talk."

Sergio nodded. "Max, these are my friends. They're good people. All of them. We can talk in front of them. In fact," he said, pointing at William and Alex, "these two may actually be able to help our cause."

Max frowned. "How?"

William stuck out his hand. Max reluctantly shook it. "I'm a journalist who specializes in the outdoors. If someone's poisoning a river, I want to know about it."

"You write about the outdoors? I'm surprised you didn't know about the French Broad, considering it's one of the oldest rivers in the world."

William rolled his eyes. "It was a joke."

"Not a good one." Max turned to Alex.

"I'm also a journalist. A travel writer."

"Surprised to see you here instead of the Biltmore. Isn't that the kind of thing you people cover?" Max said, with a not inconsiderable dose of snide.

Alex's lips thinned and she inhaled deeply through her nose. "Look, Max?" Emily spoke up before she could say anything. Alex realized she must have met him on a previous visit to see Sergio. "I know you're upset, but do not talk to my friends that way, especially when they've flat out told you they want to help."

Max glared at Emily, then dropped his eyes, contrite. "You're right. I'm sorry. It's just that, that Mitchell. He's literally killing the river. I found more dead fish this morning. That's what prompted me to test the water again. I hope you two didn't drink much of his poison."

Alex and Emily shook their heads. Billy broke his silence. "Two questions. One, why are you testing the water, and two, who is Mitchell and is he dumping illegally?"

"That's three questions," William pointed out.

It was Billy's turn to roll his eyes. "I know you're trying to lighten the mood, but now's not the time," he said. Alex was amazed at how gentle Billy, the no-nonsense cop, sounded when he talked to William.

"Max here's a Riverkeeper," Sergio began.

"A what?" Alex asked.

"A Riverkeeper," Max broke in. "I monitor the pollution levels of the French Broad River."

"So what do you do? Camp by the river and take samples?" Alex was still bristling over his condescension about her career.

"Among other things, but yes, taking water samples is a big part of it."

"It's a constant battle," Sergio said. "The French Broad used to be so polluted people would say it was too thick to drink–"

" – and too thin to plow," Max continued. "We've made real progress since the Clean Water Act, but not enough. There's still too much E. coli in the water. Much of the river isn't safe to swim in, let alone drink." He turned to Sergio. "You're seriously allowing Mitchell to be part of your fundraiser?"

Sergio straightened his shoulders and squared off with his friend. "Max, we've gone over this how many times? I have a plan."

Max shook the test tube in Sergio's face. Alex was glad the Riverkeeper hadn't brought any of the dead fish he'd found. He probably would have slapped Sergio with it. "Your plan is taking too long," he growled. "I took this immediately downstream from his brewery."

"Could it have been from something else?" William asked.

Max glowered. "Don't you think I would have taken a sample from upstream? This is my job. I am not an idiot."

Sergio took a deep breath. "I know you're upset, and rightfully so, but don't take it out on my friends. Why don't we go outside and talk."

Max didn't answer. His gaze switched from Sergio to Calliope, who was turning the corner of the bar, visibly calmer than she'd been when she left. She gave the Riverkeeper a shy smile. Sergio coughed and she looked away. "Sure. Yes," Max said. "Let's go."

Sergio nodded and tilted his head towards the back door, propped open to let a breeze flow through the historic building. "Pick a spot and I'll meet you out there." He turned to the taps and filled two tulip glasses. Before following Max, he spoke to Emily. "Don't worry if you drank any of Mitchell's beer. He doesn't use the water from the river. Nobody does. It goes through a treatment plant, just like everywhere else."

"I figured," she said, then continued. "Doesn't seem like Mitchell's on too many Christmas lists."

"Ha!" Sergio guffawed. "You could say that again. Look," he said, scanning his friends. "We'll talk later. I can see Max pacing out there. I need to try to calm him down before he wears a trench in my grass."

He said the last with a grunt that was more in line with his tough guy exterior than the gentle tones he used with Emily, William, Billy, Alex, and anyone else he actually liked. Calliope watched him walk towards the creek. She glanced at the glasses on the bar, noticed they were empty, and began removing and replacing them one by one.

"I thought breweries were all nice and worked together and stuff," William said.

Alex, who'd covered the beer scene frequently and was a fan of craft beer in general, shrugged. "People are people. While yes, the industry is one of the most collaborative I've seen, there are still rivalries and bad actors."

"Seems like Mitchell is definitely one of those."

"Yes," Calliope said. "He is."

"Do tell," William prompted.

Calliope shook her head, hesitating before speaking. "I'll let Sergio fill you in. I don't want to say anything out of turn. I'm new to all this, you know." She smiled, and Alex swore a halo appeared above her head. If Alex were interested in women, she'd be begging for the bartender's number. Calliope continued. "It's a beautiful evening. Why don't you sit outside? I see an open row of chairs along the creek."

The friends took the hint. Alex picked up her glass. "OK to take this outside?"

Calliope looked confused at the question. "Of course. When you're done, there's a tub for dirty glassware."

Alex walked towards the creek, followed by her friends. She turned to talk to Emily and saw William and Billy holding hands. It made her smile. It's something she never would have guessed would happen when she'd met Billy the previous summer.

Emily looped her arm through Alex's and lifted her glass. "I feel like a rebel."

"Ditto," Alex said. "Taking glass outside? I feel like I'm breaking the rules."

"And we all know how much you like to break the rules," William called.

"What? I like order, and figure rules are there for a reason."

"Yeah, to break them."

"Well, I, for one, appreciate those who follow them," said Billy.

They neared Max and Sergio, who had moved to the banks of the creek. Max bent down and pulled out a test tube. He looked up at Sergio. "Might as well," he said, filling the tube with water.

"You need to test it even here?" Alex asked. "Even though it's mountain runoff in a National Forest?"

"It's still good to test, just in case. Plus it acts as a point of comparison," Max said. Alex studied him as he watched a pit bull jumping in the water. Droplets sprayed as the short-haired dog chased dragonflies. "See him? There are plenty of spots around here where he couldn't do that. It's not safe."

William frowned. "And this Mitchell has something to do with that?"

"He's a small fish in a big greed pond, but yes." Max remained focused on the dog. "But he's someone I can do something about," He muttered under his breath. He rattled his head as if to clear his thoughts, then turned away from the creek to face Sergio. "You think your plan will work?"

Sergio shrugged. "Only one way to find out."

Max nodded. "I do appreciate everything you're doing. I'll let you get back to your friends, but I'll see you tomorrow." He grasped Sergio's forearm and pulled him in for a hug; the two men slapped each other's backs. Alex was close enough to see Max's sleeve tattoo. It was a woodland landscape: fish jumped from a rock-strewn stream and a black bear hunched over the water in the shadow of a rounded peak covered in trees. Every time his bicep flexed, the bear seemed to swipe at the water.

Chapter 4

Max walked away. He neared a young man walking towards the creek and the two high-fived as they passed each other. Alex watched the Riverkeeper turn towards the parking lot, then her eyes followed the young man walking in her direction. He loped, keeping his head down, the hair hanging in front of his face and hiding his features. The sides of his head were shaved. As he neared the group, he shoved his hands into the pockets of his skinny jeans, which seemed an impossible feat.

"Hey Jackson, you ready to give them the grand tour?" Sergio asked.

Jackson lifted his head, flipping his hair back. "Sure thing, boss."

Sergio turned back to the group. "Jackson here's another up-and-coming brewer. He focuses on the classic styles. Got a real passion for doing it old school."

William guffawed. Billy shook his head, but smiled while rolling his eyes. "Like pilsners?" Billy asked.

Jackson nodded, his bangs bobbing up and down. "And lagers." He spoke so quietly they had to lean in to hear him.

"You've got a lagering facility?" Alex asked.

"Sure do," Sergio nodded. "Jackson'll show you around. Got your mic?" he asked the brewer.

"Yes, sir."

Alex strained to hear him, but Sergio grinned and clapped Jackson on the shoulder. "Don't forget to turn it on this time. The ladies may love your soft-spoken charm, but this group'll eat you alive."

Jackson's eyes flitted from friend to friend and Alex could see his nervousness. "Don't let him fool you," she said. "We're harmless."

"Mostly," William said. "We don't bite–too hard."

They all laughed, then William, Billy, Emily, and Alex followed Jackson towards the tall tanks at the side of the log building. Sergio peeled off and headed to the bar. "See you in about thirty and we'll grab something to eat."

Alex pulled up next to Jackson. "How did you get started in brewing?"

He flushed a little. "Sergio."

When he didn't continue, Alex eyed the awkward man. She guessed he was a recipient of one of Sergio's scholarships. Her friend had founded a nonprofit to give troubled teens and young adults a second chance. Or, as he said, a first chance, because that was often the case. Sergio'd been through the ringer himself, accused of murdering his stepfather as a teen and then spending years in juvie until he was acquitted. Even though it was self-defense, he had still struggled to find a job or receive any sort of acceptance. Few people would look past his record to see the bright and talented young man he was until a mentor introduced him to the world of cooking. Sergio had found his purpose and vowed he'd spend his life doing for others what his mentor had done for him. He'd originally planned to work only with teens, but realized young adults also needed guidance, often more.

"Was this something you've always wanted to do?"

Jackson shrugged. "Not really. It seemed like the easy way out." He grinned. "Goes to show I didn't know Sergio very well, doesn't it?"

"Sergio doesn't seem like he'd be easy about anything," William quipped. "Except maybe Emily," he said, pointing his thumb at her.

"Ha! Not on your life," Emily said. "So, you're part of The Onion Squad?"

"Charter member. Calliope and I got the first two scholarships." He blanched. "Don't tell her I told you."

Alex patted him on the arm. "Your secret's safe with us. Although I didn't realize it was a secret," she whispered.

He vigorously shook his head. "It's up to her to say. Not me. Anyway," he said, and turned towards the tanks towering above them, "these here are our fermentation vessels."

"You must brew a lot of beer," Billy said, eyeing the shining silver silos.

"Sure do, but we don't use all these, yet. Sergio planned for growth, and from the way things are going, we'll need them pretty soon." Jackson's soft voice barely carried. Emily asked him to turn on his microphone, and he blushed a little while flipping the switch on the pack attached to his belt. It squealed before he turned down the volume. "Sorry. Is that better?"

"Much," Emily said.

"So you focus on traditional styles. Seems like Calliope is more avant garde. Are you two the only brewers?" Alex asked.

"No. Sergio brews, of course. He's got his signature stout and an amazing smoked porter. We've got a few other apprentices, but they mainly focus on food. Here, let me show you our small batch area. This is where we get to experiment."

As Jackson spoke, his passion surfaced; he became more relaxed and his volume increased. He walked them through the brewery, pointing out the steps involved in brewing beer. Alex had taken so many brewery tours that she practically could have led it herself, but it was magical to see the shy man's face fill with excitement. As he spoke loudly about the hops and how he'd found sources in Europe to make his beers as authentic as possible, she tapped him on the shoulder and pointed to the microphone. "I don't think you need that any more."

He gave her a sheepish grin and turned off the lavalier. "Sorry. I'm still not used to talking to people. Sergio thought this would help."

"Seems like it works," William said, covering his ears in mock pain. Jackson looked embarrassed. "No worries, young man. I'm no stranger to shyness." The friends jerked their heads towards him. "What? I wasn't always this gregarious, confident bon vivant who stands before you today. Which goes to show you, Sir Jackson, there's hope for you."

Emily laughed. "That may not be the pep talk you think it is."

Jackson, however, relaxed. He grabbed some pint glasses and poured them each a beer. He stopped before the froth could spill over the glasses, exhibiting a care that had been completely missing from Mitchell's pours earlier that day. Alex thought about Max's accusations about the man, and realized she didn't doubt them in the slightest, and wondered what exactly Sergio had in mind to "take care of him."

The birds woke Alex up. After a night of beer and laughter she'd finally gotten back to her cabin around ten. She'd wrapped up in a fleece blanket that had been thrown across the sofa and sat outside before going to bed. While the trees had blotted most of the night sky, she had still seen sprinkles of stars.

Alex pulled a coffee mug from the cupboard and laughed. It was shaped like a female ogre: Fiona from Shrek. Sergio was a huge fan of the movie and had named his non-profit The Onion Squad in honor of the scene where Shrek explains that ogres are like onions. "Peel back the layers," Sergio often quoted, "and you find gold." It's also where the name of his brewery originated. Sergio wanted Layers to be more than just a place to drink and eat. He wanted to prove that nobody is just one thing.

Alex poured her coffee and added a little honey. Normally she used stevia, but since Asheville was not only Beer City, but also Bee City, she decided to honor the local customs.

A rustle caught her attention. She looked up to see fuchsia hair bobbing above the railing. Emily trudged up the stairs to the deck, wrapped in a blanket just like Alex had been the night before. "Got any more of that?" she asked, her voice husky.

Alex stared. Emily never got up this early. She could compete with William in that department, but her reasoning was related to her job as a restaurateur, not because she needed her beauty rest. Emily flopped into a chair and put her feet up on the edge, wrapping the blanket around her legs.

"You're catching flies over there," Emily said. Alex closed her mouth, then slowly got up and backed towards the door to the cabin, keeping her eyes on the woman sitting on her deck. Emily threw her head back and gave a full-throated laugh. "Surprised? Yeah, me, too. I couldn't sleep."

"Is Sergio...?"

"Yep. Snoring like a train in a tunnel. That man may light my fire, but I was ready to smother him."

Alex wiped her brow with the back of her hand. "Whew! I was afraid you'd been replaced with an evil clone or something. Be back in a sec." She entered the kitchen, selected a mug shaped like Donkey, and opened the refrigerator, discovering a bottle of French Vanilla creamer. She poured a liberal dose into the cup. Emily was one of those people who didn't want her coffee to taste like coffee.

Emily grabbed the mug from Alex and snorted. "He told me why he chose the names he did for his non-profit and brewpub, but didn't tell me he was going all-in." She took a sip, stretched her legs out, and eyed her friend. "You ready for today?"

Alex narrowed her eyes. "And why, pray tell, shouldn't I be?"

"Oh, you know," Emily shrugged. "A certain Riverkeeper's going to be there."

"As will a ton of other people." Alex sidestepped the implication.

"I thought I detected a spark."

Alex grunted. "Sure, because he was *so* charming."

"You hate charming."

"True, unless it's William–"

"He's in a whole other category."

"–but I'm also not a fan of derisiveness. 'Shouldn't you be at the Biltmore?' Jerk."

"Yeah, but a super hot jerk."

"Cheers to that," Alex said, tapping Fiona's nose against Donkey's ear. Emily eyed Alex through the steam rising from her coffee and smirked, so slightly Alex would have missed it if she hadn't been expecting it.

Alex got up, walked to the railing, and looked at the laconic creek. Water flowed around clusters of rocks, smoothing the edges as it had been doing for millennia. She turned to lean against the wood and brought her mug, or Fiona's mug, she thought, smiling inwardly at her pun, to her lips, blowing on the steaming liquid before taking a sip. "I'm more concerned about Mitchell. I wonder what his story is?"

"Sergio filled me in some last night." Emily stopped at Alex's raised eyebrows. "Yes, we did talk. We're not teenagers, you know. Anyway, apparently Mitchell's bad deeds go beyond polluting the water."

"Although that would be bad enough."

"You got that right. He's your typical robber baron wannabe. Snapped up what's now Monolith after giving the former owner a loan and then, shall we say, collecting. He wants to swallow all the other breweries, under the pretense of 'promoting Asheville's beer scene to the benefit of all,'" she said, using air quotes. "Nobody's buying it. Especially not Sergio. He's kinda familiar with the greedy types."

Alex nodded, remembering Sergio's stories of his step-father. She sat down and put her head against the back of her chair, looking up through the leaves. The friends sat in silence for a moment until Alex broke it. "Seems like it's going to be a gorgeous day for drinking beer."

"And for a good cause, too. I'm really proud of him. Did you see how excited Calliope and Jackson were? You'd never guess what they'd been through. Sergio really did give them a new lease. He helped them find their purpose." Emily's voice was filled with awe and a touch of wistfulness.

"How are you two going to handle this?" Alex asked, waving her hand to indicate the back and forth between the two.

She sighed. "No idea. We're taking it one day at a time. It's not like either one of us can pick up and move, or even want to. He's got Onion Squad and Layers, and I've got Elements. Did I tell you we're adding a couple more farms to our menu? I found one of them at a farmers market last weekend. Best cherry compote I've ever tasted. It's going to be dynamite on pork chops." Her face shone with excitement and her leg began to jiggle. Emily always became animated when she talked about her restaurant, especially when she discovered a new producer she could help.

Alex reached across and squeezed her friend's hand. Emily and Sergio were perfectly suited for each other, it seemed, except for the ten-hour drive between their two passions.

Emily stood, handing her mug to Alex. "I better get back. Sergio's even harder to wake up than William, and he needs an early start today." She leaned over and kissed Alex on the cheek. "See you in a few hours."

Alex watched as Emily wrapped her blanket around her and crossed the short distance to the other cabin.

Chapter 5

The line inched forward until they finally reached the front. Alex leaned out the window with the parking pass Sergio had given Emily that morning. A teenage girl with braids waved them towards a section marked VIP and Alex drove past the orange cones. "It's good to know people"

"You get this treatment all the time," Emily said.

Alex grinned. "Not *all* the time, but often." She parked right in front of a rope barrier strung between short stumps, then followed the signs towards the entrance. She inhaled. "I love that smell."

Emily sniffed. "Hops, yeast, and barbecue. Yep. This is definitely a happy place."

"Or a hoppy place!" Alex snickered.

"You've been spending too much time around William."

"Or he's been spending too much time around me."

They skipped the long line and approached the table marked Media. Emily already had a wristband from Sergio, but because Alex was working, she wanted to have a Press badge. She found people working fests like this were more likely to talk to her if they knew she was a member of the media.

She took her badge from the woman at the table, who looked over Alex's shoulder. "And you are?"

"William Blake."

Alex spun around, catching him mid-yawn. "Good morning!" she sang.

William grimaced. "It's morning, anyway," he said, then smiled. "Kudos to Sergio for starting this at a decent time.

"It *is* a beer fest. Might not be too seemly to start any earlier."

"Good thing, too," Billy said. "Managing something like this is hard enough as it is. We had a wine fest in Door County last fall and let's just say my partner and I had to wrangle a few day drinkers."

"Brought the scofflaws to the pokey, did you?" William squeezed Billy around the shoulders. "That's my big strong po-lice man."

Billy rolled his eyes. "Yeah, well, I'm off-duty today."

"Darn right you are." William took a pair of badges from the woman at the table. She also handed him tasting glasses and William passed them around. "Let's get this party started, shall we?"

They entered the festival, ignoring the curious stares of people waiting in line. Alex received special treatment from businesses and event hosts because they wanted her to tell their story. She had experienced this enough times she felt she should be used to it, but she wasn't. It always prompted her to make sure she did a great job.

Unlike most beer festivals, this one didn't have a VIP section, a VIP tent, or VIP early access. It was part of Sergio's egalitarian nature. He wanted everyone to experience the same thing. While he did offer special perqs for the fest's sponsors, that was the only concession he made. Even the admission was reasonable.

"I can't believe tickets are only $15 for this," Alex said. "Isn't he going to lose money?"

Emily shook her head. "Nope. The brewers all pay a fee to participate and bring their own beers, plus he's got corporate sponsors. He also secured a small grant, which paid the park fees and advertising. But here's the man himself."

Sergio approached them, a walkie-talkie at his belt. It squawked and he pulled it off and answered, then put it back into its holster. "Glad you all could make it. Here, let me show you around."

He was relaxed, which surprised Alex since this was the first time he'd hosted this festival, or any festival, as far as she knew. It seemed to be well run, although it was hard to tell because they were one of the first few to enter. For the venue, Sergio had chosen a city park in Asheville that was right on the French Broad River. There were plenty of tables, and a semicircle of canopies started and ended at the river, with a few gaps filled by food trucks. One of the gaps, marked by a giant arch painted with onions and steins, led from the parking area. Through another gap, Alex could see a row of porta potties. Attendees never had to go far for a beer or for something to eat.

Sergio pointed out a number of people walking around with chartreuse t-shirts. "If you need anything today, find one of those guys. They can tell you who's got what and what's where. They can also get a hold of me."

"So who's your favorite, besides Layers?" Alex asked.

"Now, you know I can't tell you that."

"I bet it's not that one," William said, pointing to Monolith. Their canopy took up two spaces. Behind the white peaks, Alex saw a small trailer, and behind that, a large RV. Although much of it was hidden, she figured it was one of those rigs that would comfortably accommodate a family of six.

Sergio didn't respond. "C'mon. Let's go say hi to Calliope. I want to make sure you get a taste of her beer. I wouldn't be surprised if she runs out today."

They followed him like a row of ducklings. Calliope grinned when they approached. One by one, they gave her their tasting glasses and she filled them, then waited while they sipped.

"So, you going to tell us what the secret ingredient is?" Alex asked. "It's earthy, yet almost floral."

She beamed. "Marigolds."

Sergio reflected her smile. "She grew them herself. I'm sure Jackson showed you our garden during your tour? They're all growing ingredients to use in their beers. This one thought marigolds would be a good idea."

"Oh, she was so right. I've never tasted anything like that." William handed his glass to Calliope. She looked at Sergio, and when he nodded, she refilled the taster. "I don't need to go any-where else today, thank you very much," he said.

They laughed, interrupted by another squawk on Sergio's radio. "Boss, you need to get here now."

Sergio snatched it from his belt. "Where's here?" he growled.

"Monolith."

Sergio glared at the radio and swore under his breath. "On my way."

"We're following him, right?" William whispered.

Sergio called without turning around. "Of course you are."

"It's so precious you still think you can whisper," Emily said.

"That's because *he's* so precious." Alex followed Sergio and turned around to wave on her friends. "Get the lead out, Mr. Blake, if you want any chance at all of finding out what's going on."

"My my. You've gotten sassy, Miss Sassy Pants."

"Darn right I have." Alex narrowed the gap, slowing down as she neared Sergio so she wouldn't run into him. Greg Mitchell stood toe-to-toe with Jackson, practically knocking the young man over with his gut. Jackson's scalp, visible under the tightly shorn hair above his ear, was beet red. Alex could feel the heat of his anger.

"Get this... this delinquent away from my tent," Mitchell shouted, spittle flying from his mouth. He pushed Jackson. The young man fell, bracing his impact with outstretched arms. He flopped his bangs back from his eyes and leapt up, about to attack Mitchell when a large hand clasped onto Jackson's shoulder.

"Who're you calling a delinquent?" asked a deep, rumbling voice. Alex recognized the man she and Emily had met the day before after driving the Tail of the Dragon. Instead of attire suitable for skidding a motorcycle, he wore a neon-green t-shirt and pink camo cargo pants. He pulled Jackson back and stepped in front of him.

"Roger?" Alex asked.

"Told you you'd see me. Kinda hard to miss in this," he said, tugging his shirt. "Greg, you back off Jackson or I'll show you what a delinquent is."

"What are you doing here? You're not supposed to be within 25 feet of me," Mitchell stuttered. "Sergio, I knew you hired criminals, but this, this felon takes the cake."

Sergio stormed up to Mitchell. "Now you listen to me, you weasel. I let you be part of this because I thought I'd show you how real breweries treat each other, but you lay a hand on my people again, if you even *look* at them the wrong way, I'll kick you out faster than people dump your beer."

Mitchell's eyes darted, trying to find an ally. None appeared. His eyes shifted between Sergio and Roger, ending on Sergio. "You need me, remember? Besides, he started it," he said, pointing at Jackson, who was wiping grass off the seat of his pants.

William guffawed, not even bothering to hide his scorn. "Seriously, dude? What are you, three?"

Sergio put his hand up to stop William from saying any more. He didn't take his eyes off of Mitchell. "I've got this, William. Now, Greg, care to tell me what's going on?" He waited for Mitchell to respond.

"That, that weasel told me my beer was crap."

Sergio turned to Jackson, who shrugged. Emily spoke up. "He's not wrong."

Mitchell glared at her. "You. I recognize you."

Emily laughed. "Kinda hard not to," she said, gesturing to her fuchsia hair.

He faced Sergio again. "You sent spies to my brewery? I thought we had a deal."

"Spies? That's rich, man, even for you. It's a public place, and, not that it matters, but I had no idea they were going to Monolith. I've been a little busy," he said, waving his arm at the festival surrounding him. People were pouring through the arch into the open field, referring to their phones. The night before Jackson had told them he'd created an app for the festival, allowing attendees to find their favorite breweries, rate beers, connect with other attendees, and even pre-order food from the trucks that circled the field. "Look, I don't care what happened, but this is not the time or the place. Jackson, I'm sure we're busy enough that you won't need to come back to this tent, right?"

Jackson nodded. "Not a problem, boss."

"What about that one?" Mitchell asked, pointing to Roger.

"What *about* this one?" Roger growled, his arms crossed over his chest.

"You owe him an apology, Greg," Sergio said. Alex watched the back and forth. She'd known Mitchell was a bad actor, but she didn't expect to see a confrontation at a fundraiser.

"Him?" Mitchell shrieked. "I owe him nothing of the sort."

"Sure you do, or I'll sue you for slander," Roger said calmly.

Alex, Emily, William, and Billy snapped their heads towards the burly man. He winked at them.

"Sue me? For what?"

"Slander. A false statement, usually made orally, which defames another person. I am neither a criminal nor a felon. In fact, I put them away. Or at least I used to." Roger gave a slight nod to Billy.

William looked at his partner. "What's that about?"

"Like recognizes like," Roger answered. "I know a cop a mile away." He turned back to Mitchell. "If I remember correctly, and I do, your attempt to file a restraining order against me failed due to, what was it," he drummed his finger on his chin. "Oh yeah. Lack of evidence. So if you don't mind, Sergio, I'm going to keep an eye on this one today and make sure he behaves himself."

Sergio looked down, unsuccessfully trying to hide his smirk. When he spoke, it was calmly. "That won't be necessary. Will it, Greg." It wasn't a question.

Mitchell gulped, his face flushed with anger. Perspiration dotted his forehead, despite the cool temperature. "Just keep him away from me," he pointed to Jackson again.

"No problem, man. No problem at all," Jackson said, then walked away.

Chapter 6

Sergio watched Jackson as he loped towards Layers' tent with hunched shoulders, then he leaned in, pointing his finger an inch from Mitchell's face. "I better not hear one more complaint about you, Greg. I don't care how much money you throw around," he growled, then moved in even closer. A crowd had formed around them, the onlookers holding their tasting glasses and stretching to hear the conflict. Most of them had their cell phones out, undoubtedly recording every moment of the tense exchange. "These are good people, *my* people, and you will treat them with respect."

Mitchell's face whitened. Like all bullies, he was a coward, Alex thought. He gulped again. He straightened up, then glared at Sergio. "This isn't the last of this, Menendez. You better watch yourself," he hissed.

Roger laughed. "My god, you're a peach. You realize you've got at least a dozen witnesses to you threatening him, don't you? You may have money, but you sure don't have any sense." The large man shook his head, then addressed the onlookers. "Alright folks. Show's over. How about we go drink some beer? Follow me, and I'll show you where the good stuff is."

He winked at Alex before taking off in the direction of Layers. She watched in awe as the crowd followed him like he was the

Pied Piper of beer. Mitchell glared after him. Sergio leaned back, putting his hands on his hips. "You can threaten me all you want Mitchell. You don't frighten me. But you, however, should be afraid of me."

Mitchell blanched. Sergio began walking away, then stopped and motioned to his friends. "C'mon. Let's get some fresh air before I..." He trailed off, deciding against articulating what he really wanted to do. Alex stood still for a moment, watching Sergio return to his role as the affable host. She then turned to study Mitchell. The stout man's eyes narrowed as he watched Sergio walk away with Emily, William, and Billy.

"I will end you, Menendez," he said under his breath. He suddenly noticed Alex. "Did you get all that? I hope when you write your story you tell the truth."

"I always do."

He nodded. "Good. I expect to see a full accounting of what a bully he is. What bullies they all are." He walked around the tent to the large RV parked behind it.

It wasn't until he disappeared around the side that Alex turned her attention towards the tent itself. She noticed Todd wiping down the taps. He looked up at her, but didn't say a word and went back to his task. She thought about using one of her tasting tickets and started walking towards Todd, but he shook his head. "You know better," he said, then went back to cleaning the sparkling handles. She nodded to the bartender, then turned and started toward her friends.

Alex hadn't gone more than a few steps when she heard low conversation behind her. She pulled out her phone and put it up to her ear, acting like she'd received a call. Turning slightly, she saw Todd had moved to the corner of the trailer. His head was bowed towards another man. Alex recognized Vernon, Monolith's head brewer. He was the reason she'd wanted to visit the concrete warehouse the day before. She'd researched Asheville's brewery scene to prepare for her visit and come up with story ideas and discovered that until the last year, Vernon Grotto had been an up and coming brewer with an impressive string of credentials. Suddenly, he disappeared, only to appear months later on Monolith's website. Alex wondered what had caused him to take a job with Mitchell.

She spoke into her phone, continuing the ruse. It buzzed and she pulled it away from her ear. A picture of William pointing to his watch caused her to laugh. Vernon and Todd looked up at the sound. Alex smiled, talked into her phone again, and waved to Todd as she walked towards the other side of the oval where her friends waited.

Halfway there, she stopped and looked around the festival. Every brewery had a line but one.

"Welcome back. I thought we'd lost you," William said.

"You could never lose me, no matter how hard you try."

"Sassy. I like it." William pointed to Alex's empty glass. "You need to do something about that, though."

Alex got in line. "Where'd Sergio go?" William pointed towards the river. Sergio stood at the water's edge. A man stood next to him, his arms crossed, and Alex could tell even from behind it was Max. "What's up with those two?"

Emily turned Alex so she was facing the other side of the festival. "I have a feeling they're conferring about that." Emily pointed to the neon sign above the concrete slab Mitchell called a brewery.

Alex turned back to the two men and started walking towards the river, but the line she was in moved, putting her at the front. She absentmindedly ordered, her attention focused on Sergio and Max. The Riverkeeper pulled out another test tube—he must carry a case in those cargo pants, Alex mused. He scooped up some water, pulled a strip of paper from another pocket, and inserted it into the tube. She could feel their tension, even though she was several yards away. Max stood and the men faced each other. Sergio studied his feet while Max gestured wildly. Alex took her beer from the bartender, then started walking towards the two like she was drawn by a magnet. She'd gotten within a few feet when she heard Max curse.

"I'll kill him. I swear to God I'll kill him."

Alex froze. The abrupt movement caught Sergio's attention. He gave her a look that told her not to come any closer. "Tone it down, man," she heard him say.

Max grunted. "Why? I'm not the first person to say it, and I certainly won't be the last."

Alex backed away, then turned and slowly headed back to Emily, William, and Billy. She shook her head to stop them from getting closer to the two men.

"What's that all about?" William asked.

"I have no idea, but I get the feeling it's nothing good." She shook herself off, watching as Sergio threw his hands up and walked away, leaving Max staring after him. The Riverkeeper turned his head slightly. He focused on Alex, then shifted his attention back to the river. A man in a canoe floated in the middle. She watched as a group of people in inner tubes neared him. As they got closer, he pulled out a cooler and she could hear him offering them tamales for two dollars, or three for five. The noise of the festival drowned out their response, but she could see him digging into his cooler, handing over wrapped bundles, and accepting their cash. She smiled. It was an idyllic scene on what was mostly an idyllic day, with the exception of Mitchell's hissy fit and Max's obvious anger.

"I also get the feeling it might be none of our business," Alex continued.

"Is there such a thing?" William asked. "We're journalists. It's all our business."

"Believe it or not, we don't need to know everything."

"What kind of a reporter are you?"

"A thirsty one," Alex said, wiggling her empty glass. "Ready to drink some more beer?"

"Thought you'd never ask."

Chapter 7

The friends decided to split up; William and Billy saw an Ethiopian food truck with their names on it on the opposite side of the fest, nearer to Monolith. They headed in that direction, while Emily and Alex made their way around the oval, stopping at several tents. Alex had researched most of the participating breweries, but she hadn't given herself a set schedule. There were a couple she knew she wanted to try, but the rest were open.

It was a gorgeous day, with blue skies and, in the mid-70s, the perfect temperature. They'd nearly made their way back to Layers when Emily stopped, staring at one of the tables in the middle of the field. Alex followed her gaze and saw Sergio hunched over, talking to a woman, their foreheads nearly touching. She could feel the tension emanating from Emily.

"Who's that?" Alex asked.

"That is Candy. Candace. Whatever. She thinks she 'can' have anyone she wants, including him."

"Oh."

"Her last name's Mitchell."

"Double-oh." Alex studied the pair. "They don't look too cozy."

Emily's lips thinned. "Good thing. I know they have a past, but I don't know what."

"As in...?"

"I don't know. He never told me." Emily sighed. "She came into Layers the first time I was here. Sergio introduced me, said he'd be back, then ushered her outside and stayed out there for at least half an hour, leaving me twiddling my thumbs. He never did tell me why or what happened. I nearly left right then and headed straight back to Chicago."

"Why didn't you?" Alex was genuinely curious. Emily had no patience for being treated poorly by anyone.

"He made it up to me," she smiled wryly. Sergio looked up, saw Emily watching him, and winked. "And it looks like he's going to do it again."

"So you don't think he's—"

"I don't think anything. Even if he were, we see each other, what, once a quarter? It's not like I have any claim to him."

"True, but if they are, it's not cool to talk to her while you're here. Especially since she's married to Mitchell."

"Since when did you get all judgy?"

Alex shrugged. "I'm merely saying that someone who would marry someone like Mitchell doesn't seem like someone Sergio would take seriously."

Emily sipped the last of her beer and considered the couple. "Now that you put it that way... I am curious, though, what the deal is. Think you can find out?"

"Me?"

"Of course, you. You've got that thing," Emily said, wiggling her fingers, "whatever it is that makes people talk to you. I swear you know more about me than anybody alive and that's only because I can't stop myself from telling you everything. It's exasperating."

Alex wrapped an arm around her friend. "I promise to use my powers for good." The friends laughed. It was a statement Alex made any time the subject of her unique ability to get people to share their secrets came up.

Alex looked around the festival. It had grown increasingly crowded, until every picnic table and every hi-top was full. She noticed the table where Sergio and Candy— Candace?—had been standing was now occupied by a pair of couples unwrapping tacos. Alex swung her gaze around the tents, catching a glimpse of William and Billy waiting in line. Crews of green-shirted volunteers kept the grounds clean. There were no overflowing trash cans, as was often the case at festivals like this one. A huge line extended from Layers and she saw Jackson and another young man and woman she didn't recognize. She looked for Calliope, but didn't see her and figured she was probably taking a break.

They spent the next hour or so making their way to the various breweries. Whenever she had a chance, Alex asked if the head brewer was available and tried to get a moment with her or him. She was pleased to see this collection wasn't the normal bro-fest she'd come to expect. In recent years, the whole industry had become more diverse, with growing numbers of women and people of color owning breweries and creating the beer. She shouldn't have been surprised that Sergio would want that diversity represented, because she had no doubt that was something he would have insisted on.

"What do you think of that one?" A woman leaned on the table-top taps and pointed her finger at Alex's glass.

"Interesting." When the woman raised her eyebrows, Alex continued. "In a good way. Basil bitter. I've never tasted anything like it." The woman's eyebrows lifted another notch. "Also a good thing," Alex laughed.

"Same for this one," Emily said, hoisting her nearly-empty glass.

"We're all about botanicals. We work with a local farm, so when I get a crazy idea, they let me experiment. If it turns out, they know I'll order from them exclusively."

"Sounds like a good arrangement. Have you thought of growing your own?"

"You mean like Sergio? Nah. Too much work. Love what he's doing with those kids, though." She snorted. "Kids. I'm not much older than most of them. They seem so young, though."

"And yet, so old," Emily said, her voice laced with sadness.

The brewer nodded. "They've been through a lot. What Sergio's doing for them is, well, that's why I'm here. I just hope he's able to get that co-op off the ground."

Alex and Emily eyed each other, then Alex spoke. "Co-op?"

"Oh—I thought you would have known, you being his special friend and all," she said, indicating Emily.

Emily actually blushed, her face nearly reaching the same shade as her hair. She shook if off and her color returned to normal. "He's talked a bit about it, but not in detail. I gather it's a way to keep that behemoth from swallowing all of you?" Emily asked, glaring at Monolith. They were only three tents away from Mitchell's canopy. Every time Alex looked in that direction, the giant sign filled the horizon and she had to look away.

The brewster moved aside to let one of her staff continue pouring drinks for the line of patrons, then leaned forward. "Exactly. If we combine forces, we can keep him from doing here what he's done elsewhere."

"Think it'll work?"

"We've got the numbers, I think." She shrugged. "There are a few who just see dollar signs, like Vernon," she said sadly. "He's the last person I thought would ever sell out to someone like Mitchell.

Just goes to show you don't really know someone." She glanced at the line. "Sorry ladies. I need to get back to it. Nice to meet you both."

Alex and Emily decided to skip the last few tents before Monolith and walked towards an empty high top. They leaned on the table and faced the river. The banks were bare of trees and Alex noticed the tubers were gone, but the man in the canoe still drifted. He waved to the two women, then turned to see if any more customers would float his way. "That co-op must be the plan Sergio mentioned for dealing with Mitchell," Alex said thoughtfully.

Emily nodded. "He's been rather tight-lipped about it, but then again, we don't exactly have a whole lot of time to chat. Most of the time we talk after we've closed up, which is in the middle of the night. I think we yawn more than speak."

"He doesn't exactly seem like the type to talk about issues, either."

Emily laughed. "You got that right. It's like pulling teeth. Understandable, considering what he's been through, but still." She narrowed her eyes at her friend. "Maybe you can teach me some of that magic you've got. Or, better yet, you can get him to spill."

"I'm sure whatever he has planned, it's something good." Alex considered her friend. "I never would have guessed it when we first met him, but Sergio really is pure gold."

"And don't you forget it." Sergio appeared behind Emily and swept her up in his arms and winked at Alex. "I've only got a sec, but I had to see what you two were confabbing about over here." He put Emily down, then shifted his gaze beyond her.

Alex followed his eyes to Max, who'd appeared at the water's edge. The Riverkeeper spoke to the man in the canoe, loudly enough that Alex could hear him. "Careful out there, man." The Riverkeeper turned and started walking away from the water, seemingly lost in thought. He saw the trio and stopped, then took a deep breath with his eyes closed. When he opened them, he gave Alex a slow smile, then continued in her direction.

"Looks like somebody's got someone's attention," William said in her ear. She tore her eyes from Max and turned to see that William and Billy had caught up with them.

The Riverkeeper neared the group. "I owe you both an apology," he said, looking at William and Alex. "I was pretty rude yesterday."

"You can be rude to me any day." William said.

"Hey now," Billy said. "I'm right here."

"And you know you're the only one for me, but you've gotta admit…" William winked at Max.

To Alex's surprise, the Riverkeeper laughed. The tension eased, but Alex's thoughts drifted to his earlier statement about Mitchell. An idea occurred to her. "What do you know about Vernon?" Alex asked.

"He's a sell-out," Max said flatly.

But Sergio frowned. "I honestly don't know. He used to make some amazing beer. When he was at Titan Brewing, it was my go-to place. Then Mitchell came in and hired him away and now he's making, well, you tasted it."

"Where'd Mitchell come from? Did he just swoop in here like some evil vampire?" William asked.

Max clenched and released his hands. "Pretty much. Came up from South Carolina. He went from town to town, buying almost all the small operations, swallowed them up, and now they're spitting out water that's barely disguised as beer. They all taste the same. And they all taste like–"

"Crap."

Max nodded at William. "Exactly."

"And he's trying to do the same thing here." Sergio looked off at the concrete mass looming behind the white-peaked tents at the end of the festival.

"There's something I don't get," Alex began. "If he's so bad, why is he here? Why did you invite him?"

"Politics," Sergio said.

"It's always politics with slime like him," Max spat.

"He's got money, therefore he has power. Power to influence politicians, who have the power to decide who can open a brewery, where they can open it, whether they can have a beer garden, whether they can offer food, when they can be open, how much space they can have, etc. etc."

"It's a hornet's nest of red tape, and Mitchell's kicking it."

"So you think he's planning on buying up all these breweries," William gestured to the tents, "and watering them down, so to speak?"

"Not so to speak. That's exactly what he's doing, and he's already started. Vernon used to be one of the best brewers around. Now he's a lackey."

Alex nodded. "I read about him in *Brews News*. That's why we went to Monolith yesterday. I'd heard such good things about him, but then he fell off the map. I was surprised to see him mentioned on Monolith's website, considering the awful things I'd heard about them."

Emily narrowed her eyes at Alex. "You didn't tell me any of that."

Alex shrugged. "I wanted you to go in with an open mind. If you knew the rumors about Mitchell, I don't think it would have gone well."

Emily grinned. "True. Speaking of which, why didn't you say anything?" she asked Sergio.

He shrugged. "Not worth speaking about."

"I'd say it is. Wait—is that why you built Layers outside of the city?"

Sergio rocked his hand. "One of the reasons. A minor one. I mainly picked that spot because it's gorgeous. And these kids need something beautiful in their lives."

Alex, still focused on Monolith, noticed one of those "kids" racing towards them. She could tell Jackson was trying to keep himself under control: every time he'd near a cluster of people, he'd slow down and give them a curt smile and nod. As soon as he was past each group, he'd pick up his pace again. Alex could see a look of near panic on the young man's face.

"Um, boss?"

The rest of them turned as one to see Jackson. He was out of breath, his normally fair skin completely devoid of color. Sergio gestured to his radio, but the young man's eyes didn't move. He looked like he'd seen a ghost. He looked *like* a ghost.

"Spit it out, son."

"Mitchell," he gulped, "Mitchell is dead."

Chapter 8

Max threw back his head and laughed. Sergio glared at him. "What?" Max said. "Looks like someone beat me to it."

Sergio tore his eyes from Max, then gently rested a hand on Jackson's shoulder. "It's alright, son. Tell me what happened. Just start at the beginning."

"OK. I went back to our tent, like you told me to, boss. Things were going great. They really love our beer, man."

Sergio waited patiently, then motioned for Jackson to continue.

"Yeah, right. So we're pouring like crazy."

"You and Calliope?"

Jackson shook his head. "Nick and Suze and me. The lines, man, they were nuts."

Sergio waited, again.

"So, yeah, anyway, we blew a keg and I went to change it and it was giving me fits, and when I got back to the front Calliope was back and she was hopping mad."

"Hopping," William repeated with a giggle. Sergio glared at him. Jackson blushed.

"She started pacing back and forth and cursing. You know how she does, but I've never seen her so angry, and boss, you know she can get mighty angry. I just stood there. 'Tastes like sewage,' she said. 'I'll show him sewage. Drown him in his own crap.'" Jackson wiped his cheek, and Alex pictured spittle flying from Calliope's mouth to that very spot. If so, she was the second person to spit on the poor guy that day. "I just waited and she stopped right in front of me. She told me Mitchell said that. Stopped her on her way back from the bathroom, looked her straight in the eyes, and said her beer was sewage. Said he didn't expect anything else from gutter trash like her."

William gasped. "Did she punch him?"

Jackson clenched his fists. "No, but I was going to. I know he said that to her to get back at me."

Sergio directed all of his attention at the young man.

"I swear boss," Jackson gulped, "that's all I was going to do. He deserved it."

Sergio shook his head. "That's not a solution, Jackson. We've talked about that."

The young man's shoulders slumped. "I know, but I couldn't see straight. It's Cal, you know? So I took off to show him what's what and that's when I saw him. Vernon I mean. He looked awful, boss. I asked him what happened, and he just pointed to the trailer, so I went in. And, and, and–" He exhaled deeply, trying to steady himself.

"It's OK, son."

William handed the young man a bottle of water and he drank it greedily. His breathing began to slow. He rattled his head and pointed towards Monolith's tent. "He's in there. In the trailer. Vernon found him."

"In the beer cooler?" Sergio asked. He began guiding Jackson across the field. The rest followed behind. Emily walked next to Sergio, near enough for him to touch her if he needed.

"No, the trailer. The RV," he gulped.

"Breathe. Just tell me what happened, step by step."

Jackson stopped. Alex had been following so closely she nearly ran into him. He squeezed his eyes shut, then opened them and focused on Sergio. "I got to their tent and saw Vernon. He was bent over and I could see he'd puked and Todd was trying to get him to drink water or something. I asked if everything was okay, then Vernon threw up again and Todd had to jump back, and I asked what was going on and Todd just shrugged and said he had no idea, and Vernon grabbed the water and drank it and just pointed at the RV and he said 'He's dead, he's actually dead.'"

"That's exactly what he said?" William asked. Sergio gave him a warning glance and William mimed locking his lips and throwing away the key.

"Keep going," Sergio urged gently. "What happened next?"

"What are you talking about, I asked him, and Vernon pointed again so I went to the RV and opened the door and that's, that's when I saw him. He was just lying there in this big puddle and it stank, it stank so bad." Jackson heaved, and while William and Alex backed up, Sergio stayed put.

"Sergio, may I?" Billy asked. When he nodded, Billy faced Jackson. "Did you step inside the trailer?" Jackson shook his head vigorously. "Good. Are you sure he was dead?"

Jackson lifted his eyes in horror. "Wait, what, you think he might still be alive?" He took off, running towards Monolith's tent.

"Crap," Sergio said, then raced after him, doing the same run-walk Jackson had done when he came over to the group to tell them what had happened. He passed Roger, who turned from a cluster of people and eyed them quizzically. Sergio motioned for him to follow, and the big man joined them.

"What's going on?" Roger asked Alex.

"Somebody killed Mitchell," William blurted.

Roger slowed. He smiled just slightly enough Alex barely noticed, then turned his head away. "Are you sure?"

"That's what we're on our way to find out," Emily said, then took off to catch up with Sergio. The field seemed to elongate as they made their way towards the brewery's tent.

A crowd had begun to form and Roger sped up. He quickly marshaled another green shirt to help him keep people away from the tent. Sergio stopped to talk to Vernon, who was still bent over, then raced around the trailer. The group's pace quickened as they neared the tent. Sergio wasn't gone more than a few seconds when he appeared around the corner and motioned for Billy.

Alex had nearly reached Monolith's canopy, but she stopped and looked up at the sky. *Not again. Please, not again.* William paused to wait for her and she rushed to catch up. Roger passed her without a glance, issuing orders into his radio. She swiveled her head to watch him for a moment, but then smelled something putrid, stopping just in time to sidestep Vernon, who was still bent over with his hands on his knees.

Billy disappeared behind the RV with Sergio. William walked over to Vernon, gently easing him away from the puddle at his feet, then glanced around until he saw an empty chair at the next tent. Alex grabbed it. William led the brewer to it so he could sit down. Billy returned and nodded approvingly, then squatted in front of Vernon. "Can somebody get him some—thanks," he said, taking the cup of water from William and handing it to Vernon. "Take a drink and a few deep breaths, then tell me what happened."

Vernon looked up, his eyes haunted. "He's dead. He's actually dead."

Sergio appeared around the corner of the RV, gently leading Jackson. He had his phone to his ear, then pulled it away and focused on Billy. "Cops are on the way. Jackson? Grab some of that cording and some stakes. Let's get this area roped off."

"Smart thinking," Billy said, then turned back to Vernon. Alex hovered nearby. The brewer seemed like he was out of danger of hyperventilating, but he still had an odd cast to his skin. She noticed spots on his shoes.

Jackson returned with the stakes and cord, calmed down now that he had something to keep him busy. "You got enough rope?" Sergio asked him, then reached into his back pocket and threw a bunch of bright green zip ties to the young man. Jackson was about to lash the cord around the last stake when Candy pushed him aside and stormed into the clearing. Up close, Alex could see lines around the woman's eyes and realized she was older than she'd first thought.

"What's happening? What are you all doing here? Where's Greg?" Candy demanded.

Sergio approached her, putting his hands on her shoulders. "I'm sorry, Candy."

She focused on him. "For what?"

"Greg is gone."

"Gone? What do you mean, gone?" she shrieked. "He can't be gone. We still have work to do. Today was going to be huge for us. Huge. He promised."

"Something's happened. I don't know how to say this, so I'm just going to say it: Greg is dead."

Candy gasped, then slapped Sergio with such force it whipped his head to the side and left an angry mark on his cheek. "Liar! You're a liar. I knew you had it out for him. You did this, didn't you?

Where is he. Show me! Show me where he is!" She began walking around the tent towards the trailer. Sergio followed, but quickly got in front of her. Alex, pulled by the tether of her constant curiosity, trailed after them. She looked down at Vernon, hoping he'd get up since he was the one to find the body, but he seemed catatonic.

They turned the corner and reached the door set near the front of the trailer. It was one of those monster fifth wheels, bigger than Alex's condo in Lincoln Park. Sergio climbed the metal steps and turned around at the top, trying to block Candy, who was so close she had to take a step down.

"Get out of my way." She pushed Sergio, knocking him off the steps and wrenching open the door and pushing her way inside.

"Nooooo!" Her scream pierced through the aluminum walls of the RV. Alex refrained from covering her ears, but William had no such hesitation. Billy rushed past Alex and entered the trailer, and she followed, William tagging along right behind her. Mitchell was strapped to a recliner with yellow rope. A wet rag smothered his mouth and nose. The floor was covered with liquid. The place reeked of beer.

"Beer boarded," William said, peeking over Alex's shoulder. "Now that's a truly awful way to die."

"Especially with that beer." Emily spoke on Alex's other side. The three corralled themselves at the end of the trailer, away from the body.

Candy stood near her husband's head, her hands covering her eyes. "No, no, it can't be. Greg," she cried. "Please Greg, wake up, come back to me."

Billy gently pulled Candy away and checked Mitchell's pulse. They all knew it was a formality.

Chapter 9

"**S** tep aside." A uniformed police officer opened the door to the RV and stopped when he saw the crowd inside. "What in blazes is going on in here? Get out, all of you." He looked down at the floor, noticing the pooled liquid. "Stop. Sit down. We're going to need your shoes." He turned to the officer behind him. "Get their info. All of them. You," he said, pointing to Billy. "Open that window and let some air in."

Billy nodded, then did as the officer asked.

"They need our shoes?" William whispered. "But I love these shoes."

"You'll get them back," the other officer said.

Alex sat in a booth in the kitchen area and scooted around a semi-circular table to make room for Emily and William.

"Hey Ortiz," Sergio said to the first officer who'd entered the trailer. The cop had taken Billy's place and also checked for Mitchell's pulse.

"What have we got here, Sergio?"

"Isn't it obvious?" Candy answered. "Someone murdered my husband." She raised a shaky finger and pointed it at Sergio. "*He* murdered my husband."

Officer Ortiz studied her, then turned to Sergio. "Is this true?"

Sergio laughed. "Sure, man. I did it. I killed him."

"I told you! Arrest him!"

Ortiz turned to Candy. "Mrs. Mitchell, why don't you let Officer Brooks here get you some water?"

Brooks gently put her hand on Candy's upper arm and led her towards the table, motioning for her to sit down with Alex and the rest. Candy perched on the very edge, sitting as far from William as possible. The officer opened cabinets until she found the glasses, then filled one with water from the tap.

"No, not that swill. In the refrigerator."

William glared at the woman until Alex gently kicked him under the table. "What?" he complained. "She's rude."

Candy ignore him as she drummed her fingers, waiting for Officer Brooks to bring her a bottle of Pelligrino.

"I'm sorry for your loss," Emily said.

The woman looked up at her, scorn written across her face. "I'm sure you are, since it's your fault he's gone."

Emily's eyes widened in shock. "How in the world could it be my fault? I just met the man yesterday."

"I know who you are," Candy said, then pointedly shifted her eyes to Sergio. She watched him hungrily. He seemed to be explaining to Officer Ortiz what had happened. Alex caught snippets, occasionally hearing Vernon's name. Sergio, Billy, and Ortiz all turned to look at the table filled with people. They focused on Candy. Sergio leaned forward and Alex swore she heard Vernon's name again.

"You're Sergio's *friend*," Candy continued.

Alex felt her friend stiffen, but Emily didn't say anything. With Candy's arrival, they were so close to each other they were touching.

"Yes, I am. We're all his friends," Emily finally responded.

"Don't be obtuse," Candy said, surprising Alex with her word choice. "You know what I mean."

Emily nodded. "Yes, I do. He didn't do this, you know," she said softly.

Candy's face turned feral. Alex wanted to pull Emily even closer to protect her. "Of course you'd say that. I know how he inspires loyalty, if that's what you call it. Look at all those delinquents he hires. Bunch of psychopaths."

Emily leaned back in the booth. She watched the other woman, then turned her eyes to the group of men at the opposite end of the trailer.

Officer Brooks pulled out a notebook and focused on William. "I'm going to need your name, contact information, and where you're staying," she said. She put a pile of plastic bags on the table. "You'll put your shoes in these."

William bent over and looked at the floor beyond the table. "You want us to walk in that? Without shoes?" he asked, pointing to the vinyl flooring. The beer had drifted to their end of the RV. It was drying, and every time Officer Brooks moved, her shoe made a sucking sound as she pulled it from the sticky substance.

"We'll get you some booties. Now, name?" She went through them one-by-one. She reached Candy.

"You know who I am," the widow growled.

"Yes, Mrs. Mitchell, but it's procedure. Please."

Candy grunted, then answered, keeping her eyes focused at the other end of the trailer the entire time.

The door opened and Roger poked his head in. "Oh, hey, Gabby."

Officer Brooks smiled, then quickly wiped the expression from her face when she noticed Candy scowling at her. "Roger, um, Mr.

Parker, could you wait outside and keep an eye out for Detective Dunlap?"

Roger kept his eyes on her, then nodded. "Anything for you."

He closed the door and William nudged Alex's leg under the table. "Romance and murder in one metal box," he whispered.

Both Officer Brooks and Candy glared at him. Sergio walked towards the table, studying his feet and trying to avoid any obvious puddles. He caught Emily's eyes, then turned to Candy. "I'm so sorry."

"You should be."

"You know I didn't kill him."

"Do I? Remember, I know what you're capable of."

Alex, Emily, and William swung their heads towards her. Emily was right, Alex thought. They did have a history together.

The door to the RV opened again, squeaking and causing Candy to wince. "I told him to fix that. All he needed was some WD-40, but could he be bothered? Of course not. Wanted someone else to do it," she muttered.

A man wearing a polo and pressed khaki pants appeared at the open door. He took in the scene, turned around, and reached out his hand. Someone behind him handed him a pair of blue booties, and he put them on while standing on the top step. He scanned the room, then turned again. "We'll need a few more," he said, then entered the RV and approached the table, handing the booties to Officer Brooks. "I'm Detective Dunlap. I need all of you to do whatever Officer Brooks says." He stopped speaking as abruptly as he started. He walked to the other end of the trailer, taking the remaining booties with him and handing them to Billy and Officer Ortiz.

Candy ripped her suede boots off and put them in the bag, glowering at Officer Brooks the entire time. She slid the booties on, then stood up and began walking towards her husband's body. The police officer stepped in front of her. "I'm sorry, Mrs. Mitchell, but you'll need to go outside." Brooks scanned the table. "All of you will need to go outside."

"But don't go anywhere," the detective called from the other end of the trailer.

Candy hesitated, then slammed open the door. It squeaked and she scowled before stomping down the stairs. Alex and the rest of her friends, except for Billy, followed her. They stood in a circle to the side of the steps, keeping their distance from the widow. Candy faced Monolith, her arms crossed.

"I have to ask," William said to Sergio. "Why does she think you did it?"

"No idea, besides the fact I can't–couldn't–stand the man."

"Doesn't seem like many people could."

"Is it because of the co-op?" Alex asked.

"What co-op?" William asked.

"The one Sergio was putting together to destroy my husband," Candy answered, still facing the brewery. She turned, her eyes sweeping the group. She slowly made her way towards them, stopping in front of Sergio. "Oh yes, I know all about your little plan."

"It wasn't exactly a secret."

Candy barked. "No joke. You and all of them were going to, what was it, 'band together for beer?' It wouldn't have worked and you know it. Greg was going to buy each and every one of you. You thought Vernon was a sell-out? In the end, all of you would have been. But don't think this ends because you murdered my husband."

Sergio rolled his eyes. "Stop with the dramatics, Candace. I'm sorry for your loss, but I didn't kill Greg. No matter how much I despised the man, I wouldn't do that to you."

Candy focused on Sergio, and for the first time, tears glossed her eyes and spilled onto her cheeks. She seemed about to say something, then looked past Sergio. Her lips thinned. Vernon had turned the corner, accompanied by another uniformed officer. Sergio walked up to the brewer and patted him on the shoulder. He had to reach up to do it.

"You doing OK, man?" he asked.

Vernon glanced at the cop. He didn't say anything.

"That had to have been awful," Emily said, "finding him like that." Vernon stayed silent. "Do you know who might have, you know?"

"That's for us to ask," the officer said.

"Candy here seems to think Sergio did it," William said, "which we all know is totally ridiculous."

The officer focused on Sergio and Alex snapped her head at William. "Really?" she said under her breath. "Sometimes, my friend, I want to search for that filter you seem to have misplaced."

Vernon finally spoke. "Candy, you *know* Sergio didn't kill Greg."

Candy smirked, an expression so brief Alex would have missed it if she hadn't been studying the woman. "No, I don't *know* that. He's capable of it; that's something I *do* know. Don't I, Sergio?"

"Good grief, Candace. Anybody who saw *Dining + Destinations* knows I killed my step-father."

"And it was self-defense," William said.

"And he was acquitted." Emily defended. Her cheeks were nearly magenta.

The officer's focus stayed on Sergio. The door to the RV opened and Detective Dunlap, followed by Billy, exited. Dunlap put his hands on his hips. "Right. I'm going to need to talk to all of you. I'm also going to need to speak to Jackson Cohen and Calliope Young," he said, consulting his notepad. "Billy, since you know who they are, can you help Officer Ortiz round them up?"

"If you'd like, Detective Dunlap, you can interview everyone at my brewery," Candy fairly purred. "It's available since all our staff is here today."

Dunlap ignored her. "Vernon, you have keys?" The man, still stunned, dug them out of his pocket and began handing them to the detective. Dunlap shrugged them off. "Officer Brooks, take this group over. I'll be there as soon as I can get a hold of my partner," he said before heading back inside.

For the first time, Alex noticed a path that cut through the trees separating the festival grounds from Monolith's acreage. She turned to face the park, which was now empty except for workers tearing down the tents.

She checked behind her. Sergio was putting his radio back in its holster, then watched the dismantling of the grounds. "What will you do?" she asked.

He put his hands in his back pockets. "We'll do a rain check. I've instructed my guys at the gate to tell everyone they can show their tickets at Layers for a free beer, and I let the breweries know we'll reschedule. They've all put too much work into this."

"Yes, how inconvenient of Greg to be murdered at your little festival," Candy sneered.

Sergio scowled, but didn't turn to face her.

"Won't that cut into your proceeds? Giving away all that beer?" Alex's eyes swept the grounds and she thought of Jackson and Calliope. "Will that impact your scholarships?" she asked quietly.

"Most people won't make the drive out there," Sergio shrugged, "and those that do will drink more than that beer, and they'll pay for the rest. Plus, it's worth it to keep people from getting mad because their day of fun was cut short."

One by one, the tents around the clearing disappeared as staff broke them down and carted off the equipment. Alex was amazed at how orderly the process had been, and at how quickly it happened. She wondered if the police would have to talk to everyone working the fest. If so, that would be a giant job.

Chapter 10

Candy walked up to Vernon and opened her arms, but he shrugged her off. A flash of chartreuse caught Alex's eye and she saw Roger cutting across the park. He stopped to watch fellow volunteers break down the arch, then walked straight up to Sergio and wrapped him in a bear hug. Sergio pulled back.

Detective Dunlap emerged from the trailer, pulling his phone away from his ear. "Officer Brooks, Detective Sato will be here in about ten. Why don't you and Ortiz take everyone over to Monolith and we'll meet you there after the techs have arrived." He noticed the new arrival. "Roger. Glad you could make it."

"I've been a little busy."

Dunlap stared at him, then gave him a curt nod. "I need you to join the others. Mrs. Mitchell has given us permission to talk to everyone in their facilities."

Roger bristled, then glared at Candy so quickly Alex would have missed it if she hadn't been looking right at him. "Fine," he said. "This is the last vendor to go. I've got Jackson and Calliope taking your stuff back to Layers," he said to Sergio.

"Wait," Detective Dunlap said. "Jackson and Calliope? I need to talk to those two." He spoke into his radio, requesting that one of the officers guarding the entrance find them and bring them to the brewery. "Keep an eye out for Max Wells, and when you find him, bring him there, too."

Officer Brooks spoke up. "I'm pretty sure I saw him down by the river."

"Be more specific. These whole grounds are down by the river."

Alex shifted her attention towards the river and saw Max walking towards them. He returned her gaze, then shifted his attention towards the crowd gathered around Monolith's tent. He flicked his eyes back towards her, then focused on Detective Dunlap.

"I suppose you'll want to talk to me," Max said.

The detective nodded. "It's routine. You were seen having a confrontation with Mr. Mitchell."

"I also threatened to kill him."

"He did *not* just say that," William gasped.

Max gave him a withering look. "No sense hiding it. He's going to hear about it anyway. Might as well acknowledge it: I loathed the man. I loathed everything he was, and his death is good news."

The entire group stared at him. Billy put his finger under William's chin and pushed up, closing his mouth. Candy marched over to Max and slapped him. "How dare you," she shouted. "He was my husband."

"That's two she's slapped today," Emily said. "Seems like someone's got a violent streak."

"And you're better off without him," Max said, ignoring the physical assault. "We all are." He thrust his wrists out. "Want to arrest me now and get it over with?"

"Are you confessing?"

Max laughed. "No. I didn't kill him. I just wanted to."

"Max," Sergio said softly. "Stop. Think of Lisa."

Max whirled around to face Sergio. "I am *always* thinking of Lisa. Everything I *do* is for Lisa. Which is why I wish I'd been the one to end his miserable existence."

"And then who would take care of her? C'mon, man. I hear you, but I also know you. You'd never kill anyone."

The Riverkeeper slumped, then nodded almost imperceptibly.

Detective Dunlap watched the interplay between the two men, then frowned as his phone buzzed. He spoke to Officer Brooks. "Sato is on his way. Take all of them to Monolith. I believe you've got most of their contact info? Good. Get the rest. All of you, sit tight. I'm sorry for the inconvenience, but I'll be over as soon as we've cleared the scene."

An ambulance chirped, warning the people who had nearly finished dismantling the arch. It drove around them and parked a few feet from Mitchell's trailer. A pair of EMTs exited and sauntered towards the RV. It was obvious they knew there was no need to rush.

William looked around the brewery with distaste. "You'd think they could invest a little money in décor. I know minimalism is a thing, but this is egregious."

"It used to be gorgeous," Roger said. He, William, Billy, and Alex sat around one of the metal high tops. Roger leaned on his elbows and Alex noticed the fine covering of ginger hair on his arms. "My wife's rolling over in her grave."

They all looked at him, surprised. "This was my wife's brewery. Magnificat, she named it." He smiled with a touch of sadness. "She wasn't being fancy—that wasn't her thing. But she did love cats."

"Ha! Magnifi-cat. Awesome. Let me guess." William drummed his fingers on his chin, then pointed at Roger. "You had a bunch of felines around here, didn't you?"

Roger nodded, his smile a little bigger this time. "You could say that. Word got around that Yasmine loved cats and people would drop them off. We ended up doing adoption weekends once a month. That's how Sergio ended up with a three-legged cat named Humphrey. He said absolutely not, but nobody said no to Yasmine." He stopped talking and stared into the distance.

"What happened?" Alex asked gently.

"She died. Two years ago. Breast cancer."

The words hit Alex like she'd been punched. William reached over to take her hand. Her face was frozen. Stoic. Roger tilted his head at her, and she swallowed. "I'm a survivor," she said, so quietly they all had to strain to hear her. "I'm so sorry for your loss." Alex hated that phrase, but she didn't know what to say. Even though she'd been through cancer and had come out the other side, she still had no idea what words to use when she encountered someone who'd experienced the devastating diagnosis, and even less confidence she could provide any comfort to someone impacted by the loss of a loved one to the disease. She always felt guilty that she'd survived.

Roger stood up, walked around the table, and hugged Alex tightly. "No, no, my dear. No need for you to be sorry. There, there." He stroked her hair, which had finally grown out to the point where she didn't feel like a hedgehog, and murmured into her ear. Alex sobbed, letting out the pain of her own experience and her sorrow for Roger.

"What's going on?" Alex heard Emily say.

"Roger's wife died from breast cancer," Billy responded.

Emily rushed over and Alex felt her friend's arms encircle her. The warmth from both one of her best friends and a complete stranger calmed her. She took a deep breath, straightened, and attempted to smile at both of them while wiping the tears from her face. "I'm fine. Thank you, both." Alex squeezed Roger's hand. "Sorry about that."

"Like I said, nothing to be sorry about." He looked around the bare space. "Yasmine would hate this place now. No life. She had plants everywhere. Look up there," he said, pointing to the exposed beams on the ceiling. "You can barely see it, but she painted butterflies, cats, unicorns, hummingbirds, you name it, all over the rafters. We had a pollinator garden outside, but these troglodytes ripped it up."

"And put in a parking lot?" William said. "Neanderthals."

"You got that right."

"You know I can hear you," Candy said. She stood behind the bar, glaring at them.

"Don't care now, do I?" Roger responded.

Max approached the table and Alex unconsciously moved away from Roger, putting space between them. The Riverkeeper looked at her face, then at Roger. "What happened?"

Alex shook her head, but didn't say anything.

"Hey Max," William said. "Hope you don't mind my asking, but who's Lisa?"

"My sister," Max answered William, without taking his eyes off Alex.

"How's she doing?" Roger asked.

"Some days are bad. Some days are not so bad. Few days are good."

Alex's curiosity burned through her, but she didn't think it was appropriate to ask. William, however, had no such reservations. "Did she get sick from the water?"

Max nodded. "It exacerbated it. Camden Park was one of our favorite spots. She loved fishing. I tried warning her not to eat anything she caught because of the E. coli levels, but she's a bit hard-headed. It got exponentially worse when Mitchell moved in. That's when the numbers went off the charts." He glared at Candy.

"Was that why you became a Riverkeeper?" Alex asked.

"No, I've been a steward since I was a teenager and read about the Cuyahoga River catching fire because of pollution. Sparked a fire under me, I tell you. But when Lisa started getting sick..."

The door to the brewery opened and they all turned, the sunlight blinding them. Alex had grown accustomed to the gloominess of the space and had forgotten it was still a bright, beautiful day. Detective Dunlap entered, followed by a stocky man with deep set lines in his forehead and slicked-back black hair. Dunlap scanned the room, then stopped at the crowded table. The only two who weren't surrounding it were Candy, who stood behind the bar, and Sergio, who was in the corner on his phone. Alex assumed he was trying to make arrangements after the day's catastrophic turn of events.

"Here's how it's going to go," Detective Dunlap said. He didn't raise his voice, and he was easily heard in the cavernous space. "We'll talk to you one-by-one, and once we're done, you can leave. Mrs. Mitchell, we'll use Mr. Mitchell's office."

Candy balked. "You can't go in there. Don't you need a search warrant or something?"

"For conversations?" Dunlap sighed. "Fine. Is there somewhere we can speak to each of you individually?"

Roger spoke up. "There's the bottling room. Unless they moved it."

Dunlap checked with Candy. "Did you?"

She gave Roger a look of annoyance and shook her head. "No. Still there."

"Great. We'll start with you, Roger."

Roger had been leaning on the table and he pushed off. He gently squeezed Alex's shoulder as he walked by. Max looked between the two of them, his eyes lingering where Roger had touched her.

Chapter 11

Alex sat on the deck behind her cabin and inhaled, willing the scent of evergreen to calm her down. Learning that Roger's wife had died from the disease she'd so recently survived rocked her. Although she'd received the all-clear over a year ago, she still had blood drawn every three months, had a mammogram every six months, and saw her oncologist once a quarter. Every time, she waited in agonizing anticipation, trying to be positive and believe that everything would come up clear. She also had to take a daily pill that put her into chemically induced menopause. The hot flashes, mood swings, joint pain, and all the other side effects made her downright angry. *Every woman experiences this, yet nobody talks about it?* she thought. Well, maybe not every woman, but near enough to count.

After the detectives had taken all their statements, Sergio and his staff and guests returned to Layers. The officers had located Calliope and Jackson, and the young man and woman rode back with Sergio. Alex knew everyone was in the brewpub, but she needed a few moments to herself.

She thought about Roger and Max. Two very different men, and they both appealed to her in very different ways. Roger was confident and charming, and she felt an instant connection to him because of his wife. He would know, intimately, what it was like to receive a devastating diagnosis and then go through treatment. She wondered what type of breast cancer his wife had, if her chemo had caused her hair to fall out, if she had to get radiation.

Alex rattled her head to clear those thoughts. She focused on the creek, soothed by the sound of the water bubbling over the rocks. Now Max was completely different. He gave off that bad boy vibe, similar to Sergio. She wondered if, like Sergio, he was also a big marshmallow under the gruff surface. He was obviously a bit of a hot head, and had trouble controlling his temper. Could he have done it? Could he have killed Mitchell?

If it was to protect his sister, Alex thought he probably could.

She sighed, then stood up and walked down the deck's steps, rounded the cabin, and walked to the brewery. Layers was closed to the public that night, so it was just their little group and the staff, whom Sergio had invited to join them. Alex entered the log building. The history of the structure enveloped her, as well as the distinctive smell of bacon. Sergio walked out of the kitchen, followed by Jackson. The two were holding large oval trays and they snagged stands on their way to the table where everyone was seated.

"Your timing's perfect," William said, patting the empty chair next to him. "Sergio's made his signature chili."

"*The* award-winning chili?"

"Multiple award-winning chili," Emily corrected.

Sergio and Jackson moved to opposite sides of the table and set their trays on the stands. They put several large crocks of chili on the table, then surrounded them with bowls filled with shredded cheese, pickled jalapenos, cilantro, diced onions, pico de gallo, lime crema, and sliced avocado. They added baskets of tortilla chips, still warm from the fryer. Alex looked around for the bacon, but didn't see it. Calliope exited the kitchen, laden with her own tray. She added small ovals ringed with potato skins to the spread. They were piled with melted cheddar, sprinkled with bacon crumbles and encircled dishes filled with sour cream and chives. After everything was on the table, the three of them sat down.

"I figured we could all use some comfort food," Sergio said, pulling his chair closer to Emily.

"Doesn't chili take a while?" William grabbed a tortilla chip, dropping it on his plate and shaking his fingers. Billy took his hand and blew on the tips.

"Careful— we just pulled those out of the fryer," Sergio said, then answered. "Usually, but I know some short cuts. It's not easy to have stew simmering all day long when you're at a competition."

Emily, who was sitting across from William, leaned over to explain to Billy. "Sergio used to cross the country competing at all these chili and barbecue festivals, and he kept winning. It's how he got on the radar for the show."

"*Dining + Destinations*?" Billy asked. "William told me that's how he met you."

Alex ladled the rich stew into her bowl, then topped it with every available condiment. She took a bite, threw her head back, and sighed. When she lowered her head again, she focused on Sergio. "You, my friend, are a chili wizard."

"It's amazing what happens when thick cut bacon and short ribs get together."

"What's that flavor I'm getting? It's something different."

The chef grinned. "I'll never tell."

"I might, if you're nice to me," Emily winked.

Sergio playfully cuffed her on the shoulder. "Not if you know what's good for you."

They all laughed. Alex looked around the table. At the far end were more of Sergio's students. She hadn't met any of them besides Calliope and Jackson, but they seemed like they all got along, at least from their body language. There was a touch of tension, but nothing like it had been when they'd left Monolith. It always amazed her how sitting around a table with good food could make things seem better. She felt something rub against her leg and looked down to see the cat. Humphrey, she believed was his name. She snuck some cheese from the bowl and held it down for the purring animal before speaking.

"I'm curious," she began, "do you know why Mitchell changed the name from Magnificat to Monolith?"

Sergio's face darkened, but Calliope was the one to answer. "Because he's lazy and cheap and greedy."

"Huh?" William muffled around a spoon full of chili.

"You went there, right?" Calliope asked Alex and Emily. When they nodded, she continued. "I don't know if you noticed the pint glasses, but they're etched with MBC—Magnificat Brewing Company. Yasmine had those made. Mitchell didn't want to have to buy more, so he changed the name to something else that began with an M."

"I'm surprised he didn't name it Mitchell," William observed.

"Oh, he wanted to," Jackson said, and chips flew out of his mouth.

Calliope glared at him. "Were you born in a barn?"

"As a matter of fact, yes." Chips lodged in the corners of his lips as he grinned.

She rolled her eyes. "He was dead set–" she paled at her choice of words, "— on naming it Mitchell Brewing Company, but Candy said no way, no how, and if he did he wasn't gettin' any from her ever again."

"Aren't you the one with the inside scoop. How'd you get that little tidbit?" William asked.

Sergio reached his arm behind Emily to pat Calliope on the shoulder. "She used to work for him, poor thing."

They all stopped eating and focused on Calliope. She sighed, loudly. She focused on the plate in front of her, then looked up and scanned the group, all eyes transfixed on her. "He was as awful as he seemed, and worse." Calliope pushed away from the table and walked outside. Jackson looked at William with disgust, threw his napkin on the table, and followed her.

"Seems like she's been through a lot," William said. "I didn't mean to upset her."

"They all have," Sergio murmured, directing his focus to the young men and women at the other end of the table. "They all have."

Alex spooned some sour cream and chives onto her potato skin. "I wonder what happened to Vernon?" she asked, before cutting a slice off the end of the spud.

"That's right. He wasn't with us at the brewery," Emily said.

"They talked to him at the tent, then sent him off with the EMTs," Sergio explained. "He was pretty shaken up."

"Big guy like that?"

"William Meriwether Blake, you are the last person I would expect to subscribe to stereotypes like that," Emily admonished.

Alex grinned. She loved how her two best friends had connected. William bowed his head. "You are right, m'lady. My mistake. His size has nothing to do with his sensitivity."

"You got that right," Billy said, eliciting laughter. The Wisconsin cop had a distinct Tom Selleck vibe, and like the actor, towered over most people.

"So you're saying size *doesn't* matter?" Emily winked.

"*Some* sizes. But for real. Forgetting the man's a bit, imposing–speaking of which, so's Roger. What's in the water around here, because this place is growing some giant men?"

"Don't ask Max that," Alex said.

"Not if you don't have hours to spare, anyway." Sergio looked thoughtful. "Vernon's interesting. I know he struggled with what Mitchell wanted to do, but he worked for him anyway."

"An enigma," William said, with relish.

Sergio shrugged. "I don't think it's anything so mysterious."

"What's surprising is how solid his brewing reputation was. From everything I read about him, it seemed he was making a big impact in the scene out here." Alex spooned another dollop of sour cream and chives and took a bite. "My word, Sergio, even your potato skins are next level."

"It's the bacon grease. We brush the skins with them before grilling." Sergio crossed his arms and sat back in his chair, rocking it on two legs. "Vernon's always been very exacting. Got the best ingredients he could find, worked with local farmers as much as possible. I think the expenses got to be too high. It's happened to a lot of us."

"What about you? You do the same thing, don't you?" Billy asked. William smiled at him, clearly pleased his partner was so interested.

"We grow a lot of our own, as you've seen. Plus I've got a lot of partnerships. I give my spent grains to a rancher and he gives me a deal on meat."

"And you probably don't have to pay them a whole lot," William said, gesturing to the staff. Jackson and Calliope hadn't returned, but the other four were still eating.

Sergio frowned, obviously offended. "Nothing of the sort. They're paid a living wage."

"This is like a school for them, right?" Alex asked.

"Yes. They get scholarships, which 'pay' for their education. Most of these kids don't have any other options. I know what that's like," Sergio murmured.

Emily kissed him on the cheek. "That's what the festival was for. To help more of them."

Sergio stood up and walked to the kitchen.

Emily watched him. "He's more upset about this than he'll admit. He talked to the kids when we got back. They're worried, of course. Most of them don't have anywhere else to go, but after working with Sergio, they should have their pick."

Alex studied the cluster at the other end of the long communal table. The seats vacated by Jackson and Calliope had left empty chairs between the other students and their boss and his friends. There were two boys and two girls—men and women, Alex corrected herself.

Their futures were in Sergio's hands. At least, that's how he saw it. These six young adults were the first recipients of his nonprofit. When Alex had learned he'd named it The Onion Squad and why, it had surprised Alex. It shouldn't have, she thought. Sergio might act like an ogre on the outside, but underneath, he was one of the kindest, most giving, and most empathetic people she'd ever met.

Chapter 12

T he next morning, Alex picked her way along the creek bed, following the narrow dirt path that connected the cabins. Humphrey padded alongside her, venturing off every few feet to investigate some scent or rustle. Alex doubted she'd encounter anyone; even though she'd gotten up later than she usually did, they'd all stayed at the brewery past midnight. They were up so late, Sergio had given William and Billy one of the cabins so the pair wouldn't have to drive back to their campsite. William said they could just sleep in Bessie that night, but Sergio tempted him with the possibility of a hot shower, an indulgence their home-on-wheels didn't provide.

Voices floated through the trees. At first, Alex wasn't sure she was hearing conversation; the birds were particularly loud, especially one insistent bluejay. She stopped to listen. Yes, there were voices. She walked quietly. Rounding a bend, she made out Sergio's tones, but she couldn't place the other voice. Whoever it was, they seemed to be having a serious discussion. Should she turn around? Humphrey was nowhere to be seen. Alex hesitated, unsure of what to do. As she tried to decide if she should continue or head back the other way, parts of the conversation filtered through.

"I didn't have a choice," the other voice said. It was slightly familiar, but Alex couldn't place it."

"You always have a choice."

"Is that what happened with your father?"

Silence. Alex could picture the glower on Sergio's face. "Step-father," he clipped, "and yes, I had a choice, and I chose to defend myself. What's your excuse?"

The man didn't respond.

"I just don't get it. You had everything going for you. You had the best brewery around. You were my inspiration." *Ah*, Alex, thought. *He must be talking to Vernon.* She resumed walking towards them.

"Seriously? I had no idea."

"What you were doing, man, you opened my eyes. I'd never really considered brewing before. I didn't see the challenge."

Vernon laughed, a rueful sound that carried through the trees. "Kinda rude, Serg. That's like me saying I never considered cooking because it looked so easy."

"Ya' gotta admit. Chefs have a lot more ingredients to work with."

"Exactly. I have to be creative, and make something delicious, with serious restrictions."

Alex rounded a bend and saw the two men sitting in a couple of Adirondack chairs facing the creek. Sergio idly petted Humphrey, who sat on an arm of his chair as if he'd been there the whole time. "Morning," she said, giving them warning they weren't alone anymore.

They looked up. Humphrey ignored her. "Morning, Alex. You remember Vernon?"

She nodded.

"I imagine I'm hard to forget, after yesterday."

"That had to be pretty horrible, finding your boss like that."

Vernon frowned. "Boss. Not any more." He shook his head. "Yeah, it was awful. Plus I ruined my favorite pair of shoes."

That seemed like an incongruous thing to say, but Alex had met enough people who'd experienced traumatic situations to know not to make any hasty judgments. She neared an empty chair and motioned to it. Sergio gestured for her to take a seat. "Sergio told me your brewery was his go-to place."

Vernon smiled sadly, then focused on the creek. "*Was* being the operative word."

"What happened?" she asked softly.

The brewer shrugged. "Life." He pushed up from his chair, then turned to Sergio, who stood up and shook Vernon's hand. "Like I said, I don't know what plans Candy has for MBC, but I'm trying to sway her to join the co-op. Maybe with that bastard gone, we can get back to focusing on the important stuff." He nodded curtly at Alex, then walked away from the creek.

Sergio's eyes followed him, then he sat back down and slumped in the reclining chair.

"You're up early."

Sergio turned his head to her without raising it from the back of the chair. He pointed his thumb in the direction Vernon had walked. "He sent me a text at seven this morning saying he needed to see me. Believe me, I was not happy about it."

"Nor was Emily, I bet," Alex smiled.

Sergio laughed. "You got that right."

"What's all this about a co-op? I heard some yesterday, but I'd love to learn more."

"Always the journalist, aren't you? Let's grab some coffee inside and I'll fill you in."

The screen door creaked open before slamming shut behind Emily. "There you are." She yawned and wiped sleep from her eyes. "I woke up and you were gone," she pointed her gaze at Sergio, then shifted to Alex, "and you weren't on your deck. I thought I'd been abandoned."

Emily reached the bar where Alex and Sergio sat. Sergio spread his legs, grabbed her, and pulled her in. "Never."

Alex cleared her throat, and the two pulled away from their kiss. "Sergio was just telling me about the co-op."

"It's a brilliant concept, which this numbskull finally told me about last night." Emily nipped his nose.

"Do you really think you can get all these breweries to work together?" Alex asked, ignoring their interplay. "I'm sure they're independent because they're, well, independent."

Sergio shrugged. "So far most of them have been on board. It's not like we're going to be in each other's business. We're hoping to build economies of scale, like the big boys. You know, if we buy at least some of our ingredients in greater quantities, we'll get a bigger deal, which'll cut our costs."

Alex nodded. It did sound like a good idea, even though the logistics would be challenging. "Who'd run it, because there's no way you'd have time. Seriously, Sergio. You've got a restaurant and a brewery and a non-profit with inexperienced kids all rolled up into one."

He grinned. "Yup. Sure do."

Emily grasped his hand. "When you care enough, you find a way." The Chicago chef had her own non-profit, dedicated to connecting independent restaurants like hers with local farmers and other producers. Sergio's co-op concept was very similar, and Alex figured Emily had inspired him.

"I'm not doing it alone, though. Roger's been taking care of most of the details. He's been around a lot longer than I have. He did a lot of ordering for his wife, so he knows the players."

At the mention of Roger's wife, Alex's expression sobered. "Did you know her?" she asked, so quietly Sergio had to lean forward.

"Yes. She helped me get my start in brewing. My word, that woman was passionate. She could talk for hours about beer's history, its importance, its future, and if she stopped you'd beg for more." Sergio paused. "Her body wasn't even cold when Mitchell forced the brewery sale."

Alex paled. Emily looked at Sergio, aghast. He caught her expression and grimaced. "Oh, man, I am so sorry. I wasn't thinking."

Emily glared at him. "No, you weren't." She moved to hug Alex, but she shook her head.

"It's OK. No, really, it is. I can't expect everyone to tip-toe around me forever."

"We're not everyone."

Alex smiled at her friend, whose cheeks had turned nearly the same color as her fuchsia hair. She always got flushed when she was angry. Or happy. Or indignant. Pretty much any time Emily had an emotional reaction, she had a visceral one, too. "No, you are not," Alex agreed. "But I know I'm a bit of a minefield, and I don't want anyone, especially my friends, to be afraid of how I'll react. That would be worse." She gave them an encouraging smile. "So, Mitchell pulled the rug out from under Roger right after his wife died? That's low."

"That's Mitchell. He'd offered to help Roger keep the brewery afloat while Yasmine went through treatment. It went on for a couple years, and by the time she passed away–" Sergio stopped. He looked at Alex, and when she nodded that she was fine, he continued. "By that time, Mitchell practically owned the place anyway. Roger signed anything Greg put in front of him."

"Weren't you telling me they had a past, even before Yasmine got sick?"

Sergio nodded at Emily. "Yeah. Roger worked for Mitchell in Charleston. He was basically his axe man. He'd scout out smaller breweries and point out which ones were ripe for the picking."

Alex's jaw opened. "How can you trust him? How can you even talk to him?"

"It was years ago. Decades. Then he met Yasmine. People change. If I didn't believe that..." Sergio gestured around the historic lodge filled with tables, an old-fashioned jukebox, and weathered photos of the men who'd built the entire camp in the 1930s. "We all make mistakes. And we're often judged too harshly when we do."

Admonished, Alex agreed. Still, this revelation about Roger was disturbing, especially since he was essentially doing all the leg-work for building the co-op.

The door swung open and Calliope entered. She stopped when she noticed the trio sitting at the bar. "Morning, boss."

Sergio checked the clock on the wall. "You're here early."

"I couldn't sleep. Thought I'd come in and roast some of those coffee beans we got in. I've got some ideas for them."

"I'm sure you do. Speaking of coffee, you want some?" When Alex and Emily nodded, he got up and followed Calliope into the kitchen.

Emily watched until the swinging doors stopped swinging.

"What are you thinking?" Alex asked.

"Just wondering what her story is."

"It's hard not to, isn't it? To know these kids are here because of something awful in their lives, and have no idea what happened. I take it Sergio doesn't tell you."

"Absolutely not. He'd never betray their trust."

The door banged open. Alex looked up, expecting to see another staff member. Instead, Detective Dunlap filled the doorway. He entered and scanned the room, followed by his partner. "Where's Mr. Menendez?"

Emily narrowed her eyes at the use of Sergio's last name. "Why?"

"Just need to ask him a few questions, Ms. Kincaid."

Sergio pushed through the swinging doors, wiping his hands on a bar towel. Alex felt the breeze as the panels swung back and forth. "Hey Leo. What's up?"

"Sergio," the Detective began. "We're going to need you to come with us."

Emily leapt from her chair. "What's going on?"

Sergio squeezed her shoulder as he walked past her. He stopped in front of the detectives, then gestured for them to lead. Instead, they stepped aside and motioned towards the door. "After you."

Alex saw him straighten his spine. He rolled his neck, paused, then turned. Calliope came out of the kitchen and froze. "What's going on?" she shrieked, repeating Emily's question and barreling towards the detectives. "Sergio, what's happening?"

"We just need to ask him a few questions, Ms. Young." Dunlap put his hand up to stop her. "Please step back. Mr. Menendez is coming with us voluntarily."

"Yeah, because he knows what happens when you don't."

Chapter 13

Alex and Emily got up and approached Calliope, standing on either side of her. Alex could feel the tension emanating from the young woman and was afraid she'd try to physically stop the detectives. Sergio eyed the three of them, and a sad smile crossed his face. "It'll be fine," he said. "Calliope, call Ethan. He'll know what to do." He looked at Dunlap, and then at Sato. "Shall we then?" Sergio walked out the door towards the waiting SUV without a glance behind him.

The three women stood motionless. Emily broke first. "What in the HELL was that?" she shouted, then spun on Calliope. "I'm assuming this Ethan person is his attorney?" Calliope nodded, mutely. "What are you waiting for? Call him."

Anger flashed on the young woman's face, but she took a deep breath before pulling her phone out of her pocket and making the call, staring at Emily the entire time. Emily's face crumpled. She put her hand on Calliope's shoulder. The young woman flinched. "I'm sorry," Emily said.

Calliope nodded curtly. "I know it's a Sunday morning," she said into the phone. "Leo Dunlap just took Sergio." She pulled the phone away from her ear. Alex could hear the man on the line because his voice was so loud.

"Dunlap did what*? You've got to be kidding me. That amateur. Fine. I'll meet Sergio at the station. Did he have his phone with him?"*

Calliope looked at Emily, who pulled out her own phone and called Sergio. They heard a buzzing and turned to see a phone on the bar. "No, it's here."

He cursed under his breath. "Bring it to the station. At least I don't have to tell Sergio not to say a word."

Alex walked away and tapped a text message to William. *Sergio's been taken by the police for questioning. Meet us at the station. Bring Billy.*

Her phone buzzed a second later. *Done.*
***

Sergio entered the lobby of the police station. He looked up, saw the crowd waiting for him, then shook his head, smiling. "You guys didn't have to throw me a party. Did somebody bring cake?"

Emily ran to Sergio and tackled him, wrapping her arms around him. She pulled back, searching his face. "I'm fine," he said. "Really. I'm fine."

The door opened again and a man with sandy brown hair came out, followed by Detective Sato, who halted and looked around the room at Alex, William, Emily, Billy, and Calliope. His gaze settled on her. "Ms. Young, how convenient. We'd like to ask you a few questions, too."

Panic crossed her face. Her eyes darted to Sergio, and Alex thought she looked like a chipmunk cornered by a hawk. He smiled gently at her. "Go ahead. We'll wait for you," he said, searching the room. They all nodded. Sergio spoke to the man who'd come out with him and Sato. "Ethan, can you join her?"

"Absolutely. As long as that's fine with Ms. Young?" She nodded. "Good. Let's make this quick, Detective Sato. I believe you've got a murderer to catch."

"What do you think we're doing?" Sato growled.

"Wasting time. But please, lead on. This will be entertaining, if nothing else."

The detective glared at Ethan, but he turned the knob and motioned them through. Calliope's eyes never left Sergio's face, the fear written on her features. The latch clicked behind them and the remaining friends stared at the spot where Calliope had been.

Alex checked the rear view mirror, again, to check on Calliope. The young woman sat behind her, staring out the window as she'd been doing since they left the station. Sergio sat in the back with her, and Emily was in the front passenger seat. Alex knew they all wanted to ask Calliope what had happened, but the young woman had turned inward. She hadn't made a sound.

Gravel pinged the undercarriage as they pulled into the driveway to Layers. Alex rolled to a stop near the main building, turned off the vehicle, and waited. They all did. Calliope opened her door and got out, gently closing it behind her before walking towards the creek. Humphrey jumped down from one of the picnic tables and followed.

"Poor kid," Sergio sighed, then got out as well. Alex and Emily followed him into the log building. By the time they reached the door, William was parking next to Alex's vehicle and he and Billy soon came inside.

The group hesitated, unsure of what to do. Sergio stood in front of the large picture window that faced the open field. One by one, they joined him to watch Calliope as she stood by the water. Even from that distance, Alex could see the young woman's shoulders shaking. After some time, she seemed to settle. Alex pulled away from her friends and walked to the creek. She stood next to Calliope, silent. They stood that way for quite some time until Calliope finally looked up from the water.

"Thanks."

Alex nodded. She didn't ask her if she wanted to talk about it. If she did, she would.

"That was awful. They kept badgering me and badgering me. *Where were you? Where was Mr. Menendez? You seem to be awfully close to Sergio, don't you?* Gawd. They were disgusting. Implying Sergio and I had a thing—as if. He's twice my age. *Where were you; where was Mr. Menendez? Where was Sergio?* Over and over, as if I'd slip up and change my answer if they kept repeating the question."

Her voice had risen with each word and her breathing increased. She stopped. "If Ethan hadn't been in the room..."

Alex waited, her hands in her pockets. She fought the urge to turn her head and look at Calliope.

"I told them exactly what happened: I was nowhere near Monolith when Mitchell was murdered." Her voice hitched. "Did they believe me? Hell, no. *Don't go anywhere, Ms. Young. We may need to talk with you again,*" she mimicked. "I don't care what Sergio says, it doesn't matter what I do, I'm never going to get a break."

Alex let her simmer. She knew nothing she said would help, at least not right now. Calliope was too raw. Whatever had happened to this talented and driven person, it had left lingering scars. As young as Calliope was, Alex imagined her trauma couldn't have been that long ago. And she knew she'd experienced trauma, even without the added clue that she was one of Sergio's scholarship recipients.

"I was eleven," Calliope said, quietly, then rattled her head. She inhaled deeply and looked at Alex, her eyes filled with pain. Alex remained silent. "But you don't need to hear all that." She paused. "Thank you for not asking."

Alex nodded. "If you ever do need to talk…"

Calliope nodded. "I know. I can tell. You'd actually listen."

"William calls it my super power."

"I can see that."

"Do you need more time alone?"

Calliope shook her head and scooped up Humphrey. The cat nuzzled her neck and purred so loudly Alex could feel the vibration. "No, let's go in. I need to tell Sergio about my interview and find out about his."

Alex and Calliope entered the restaurant. At the same time, Jackson burst through the front door and frantically searched the room. His eyes lit on Calliope and he ran towards her. He reached out to her, but she flinched, fear in her eyes, and he stopped himself, stepping back and raising his hands to show he meant her no harm. "Cal—you're here. You're OK? I heard they kept you, they questioned you. Are you OK?"

Calliope relaxed and looked kindly at the frenetic young man. Humphrey grumbled, but she ignored the cat and reached out to put her hand on Jackson's cheek. "I'm fine." When he searched her face, she reassured him with a gentle nod. "Really, I'm fine."

"Those bastards."

"They're just doing their job, Jackson."

"No, they're not. Their job is to find out who killed Mitchell, and harassing you isn't going to do it."

Calliope sighed. "They're following leads, that's it."

Jackson's eyes widened. "You *know* how this works, Cal." He swallowed and leaned close to her. This time she didn't flinch. Alex figured it had been his sudden movement that had caused her reflex reaction. "I'll go. I'll tell them I was there with you."

Calliope reared back and jabbed him in the chest. "You will do no such thing, you idiot."

"Yeah, that's not a good idea," Billy drawled. They'd all been watching the exchange with interest.

"Don't even try it," Sergio growled. "You've come too far to do something stupid like that."

Jackson's nostrils flared; his muscles tensed. He visibly calmed himself, closing his eyes and inhaling, holding his breath, exhaling, and holding again. His fists relaxed. He opened his eyes and compassion enveloped his features. "I can't let anything happen to her," he whispered.

Calliope punched him in the shoulder. "I swear, you are an idiot, aren't you? I do not need you to run to my defense. I can take care of myself."

Jackson nodded. "I know. I just–"

She softened, replying just as quietly. "I know."

The strains of violins filled the air, breaking the spell. Alex pulled out her phone and silenced the music. "Sorry about that. I've got to go. I'm meeting Max."

"Oh? Do tell," William said, leaning forward and blinking rapidly.

Alex wagged her index finger at him. "It's not that, goof. This whole Riverkeeper thing fascinates me, so I asked him if he'd be open to an interview." She looked at Calliope and Sergio. "It also might help me get a better handle on what's happening here.

Speaking of that, Sergio, would you have time to talk later? I've got questions about your co-op."

Sergio crossed his fingers in front of him, as if he was warding off an evil spirit. "Oh no, you wizard. I remember what happened last time you had 'questions' for me. Had me spilling my guts before I even knew I'd opened my mouth."

"And that turned out OK, didn't it?" Alex said, pointedly looking at Emily.

He grinned. "It sure did. Yeah. I'll be around, unless I get pulled into the pokey again."

"Don't even joke about that," Calliope said, hotly.

Alex wondered for the umpteenth time what had happened to her, and to Jackson, but she also knew it was none of her business. Unless, of course, whatever secrets their past held were the key to finding out who killed Mitchell.

Chapter 14

Alex trailed her fingers in the cool water. Trees crowded the slopes that led down to the river. Mist appeared in the folds between the peaks. Smoky Mountains was an apt name for these ancient hills, worn down over millions of years from jagged summits to smoother swells. Max sat behind her in the double kayak, the rhythmic sounds of his paddles soothing her.

"We're going to pull up on that beach," he said. "It's a popular camping spot."

Max steered the kayak to the sand, moving forward until the boat stopped. Alex extricated herself from the vessel, feeling awkward as she watched Max leap out like he did this every day of his life, which, of course, he did. His shorts exposed his long legs; she swore she could see every sinew. The feeling that rippled through her body shocked her. It had been so long since she'd felt any attraction to anyone she had begun to wonder if her cancer had turned off her ability to experience desire.

Nope. Definitely not the case, she thought. She found herself staring at his back as he pulled the kayak up the bank. She shook her head and looked around the campground to keep herself distracted. It was basically a clearing with a metal fire ring and a picnic table, which looked surprisingly new.

"We just added that last week. Part of a project we've got to improve these campsites. If we can increase the number of people who use the river recreationally, they'll feel more protective of it."

"That makes sense," Alex said. She ran her hand along the table top. Instead of wood, it was made of plastic. "How many campgrounds are there?"

"Along the river? Around twenty. We don't want too many. Can't have this turning into an amusement park, you know? It's a balance. Encouraging outdoorsy types to take advantage of this beauty, while hoping it doesn't get too crowded."

Alex nodded. She watched the river. The island where they'd stopped was in a stretch with boulders that had been polished smooth. Eddies of foam pooled as the water flowed over and around the rocks. They weren't rapids, by any stretch, but they'd carry a canoe or a kayak downstream with very little effort.

She sat on the bench facing the water and tilted her head back, soaking in the early summer sun. Max sat down next to her; she felt the seat shifting just slightly with his weight. She shifted to focus on his determined face. "I can see why you love the river."

He was silent for a few beats before speaking. "I feel connected. To everything. This river's one of the oldest waterways in the world; can you believe it? Every time I get out here, I imagine what it was like hundreds, even thousands of years ago. It's worth protecting."

They listened to the gentle sounds of the water: the lapping at the small beach, the gurgles as it found its way around the obstacles in its path. With every drop, the water eroded a little more of the rocks. Alex wanted to be like that water, where obstacles were merely something to flow over and around, where her mere passing smoothed the edges. She felt like her cancer had been one of those giant rocks that seemed impenetrable, solid, like it wouldn't budge. It blocked her way. And yet, here she was, cancer free. The process seemed to take forever when she went through it, but at least it wasn't millennia. She laughed softly to herself.

"What's funny?" Max asked.

"Perspective. I was just wondering how long it took the French Broad to wear down that big boulder. It probably started like one of those." Alex pointed to a craggy ridge on the other bank.

"Water's pretty powerful."

She nodded.

"So, what amused you about that?"

Alex hesitated before speaking. "I had cancer."

Max closed his eyes, then reopened them and looked directly at her, almost through her. "And at the time it felt impossible."

She swallowed, willing the tears not to come this time. When would she be able to talk about this without getting emotional? *Stop it*, she said to herself. *You will always be emotional about the biggest thing that's ever happened to you, and that's OK*. Max adjusted his position on the bench next to her and his fingers brushed hers. A spark shot up her arm, infusing her entire body. Alex looked at him. Was this the same man who'd been so dismissive of her the day they'd met? She moved her hand away from his, but gave him a small smile. "Yes. Impossible. But I got through it."

They turned their gazes back to the water. It was hard to believe the river had been so polluted, and in some places, still was, that it made people ill. Alex thought about Max's sister. "I'm sorry about Lisa."

Max stiffened and Alex wondered if she shouldn't have said anything, but then he spoke.

"It happened so suddenly. She'd always been strong. She's a tomboy, a trait Dad blamed me for. He wanted his girlie-girl, a doll he could show off to his colleagues." Max barked out a laugh. "He should have known better. If he wanted frills and lace, he shouldn't have married Mom. Which apparently she thought, too, since she left him." He leaned forward, resting his elbows on his knees, remaining focused on the river. "Lisa got bronchitis a few years ago and it wouldn't leave. She started losing weight. They took test after test after test, finally discovering she's got this rare autoimmune disease. But that didn't stop her. She kept hiking, and kayaking, and swimming, and it finally caught up to her."

"Is she...?" Alex asked quietly.

"She's still alive, if that's what you're asking. Problem is, every time she starts to feel stronger, she overdoes it."

"I can relate to that."

"I bet. You don't seem like someone who'd sit still for long." He stood up and walked a few feet away, then bent down to pick up a piece of trash, so small Alex hadn't noticed it.

She was almost afraid to ask him the question that had been nagging at her, but she did it anyway. "Why do you blame Mitchell?"

Max turned to her, his eyes cold and fierce. "Because he and others like him have been killing the earth and this river for their own profit, and now they're killing my sister. You know where the festival was? That park was Lisa's favorite spot to enter the river. Said she loved starting there so she could see the industrial slabs give way to Mother Nature."

"And since he's been dumping in the river, the water was poisonous?"

"He and others like him. It's been going on for years. But Mitchell was literally dumping sewage into water where people, dogs, wildlife, anything alive, swim, eat, and drink. People fish along the bank and then eat what they catch, and when they do, they're literally eating his shit." The anger steamed from every pore of his body. "But not any more. Someone took care of that. Not that it'll do any good."

Alex understood his anger, but it still made her feel uncomfortable, especially since she was alone with him in the middle of a river, far away from help if she needed it. Her concern must have shown on her face, because he caught her expression.

"I didn't kill him," he said.

She kept quiet.

"I wanted to. Oh God, I wanted to murder that SOB, but who'd take care of Lisa? Dad's off in California—moved there right after the divorce—and Mom died a few years ago. Cancer," he said. He studied her, his face creased with sorrow. "I'm sorry you went through that, but I'm glad you survived."

"You and me both. Also, glad to hear I'm not stranded in the middle of nowhere with a murderer."

Max laughed. "No worries. You are perfectly safe with me. Underneath this," he said, gesturing to his tattoos and his physique, "I'm an old softie."

"Good to know," Alex said. She thought of Sergio, and how he'd also had an edge of danger when she'd met him. Now that she knew him, however, she knew his kindness. Still, if anyone hurt the people he loved, he could be quite fierce. Max was obviously the same way. "So, who do you think killed him?"

"Take your pick. Anybody at any of the breweries, or at least, most of them; anybody who cares anything about the environment; anybody who'd ever worked for him; anybody whose business he'd shut down; his wife—"

"Candy? Why do you say that?"

"What is it they say? Always look at the spouse?" He shook his head. "It's more than that. She's a gold digger and Mitchell fancied himself a ladies man." Alex nearly choked. "Exactly. The man had an ego bigger than Mt. Mitchell. You met Candy, right? Not exactly hard on the eyes. Not my type, but she's a lot of men's type. Rumor had it that's why Vernon jumped ship and signed on with Monolith."

Alex thought back through the interactions she'd witnessed between Mitchell's brewer—former brewer, she amended—and Candy. She thought she'd sensed something, but it was hard to tell with Vernon's reaction to finding Mitchell's body. "I wonder," she started.

"Yes?"

She shook her head. "It's nothing." What had popped into her head was a nascent idea: could Vernon have killed Mitchell because Candy asked him to? Maybe she promised to share the brewery with him. Alex would have to find a way to talk to him. Despite Sergio's protestations that he would be fine, she'd seen several people wrongfully accused during her time as a reporter in Chicago. She had a good feeling about Detective Dunlap, but when it came to her friends, Alex was not going to take any chances.

Alex checked her phone. She didn't have any service, but the clock still worked. "OK if we head back? I'm supposed to meet Roger."

At the mention of the other man's name, Max's face closed up. "Fine." He nodded curtly, then began turning the kayak around so they'd be facing the right direction. Alex rushed over to help, but he waved her off. He didn't say another word until they got out of the boat at the landing place where they'd started. Max reached out his hand to help her out of the kayak, holding on to hers longer than necessary. She searched his face, but his eyes were still cold. "I can understand why you're meeting Roger, but be careful."

Alex tilted her head. "And just why am I meeting Roger?"

Max released her hand and put his in the pocket of his cargo shorts. He looked down at his feet. "Because you two had a connection. I could see it."

Alex scowled at him. *Unbelievable.* "Or maybe it's because I'm a writer and he's helping to build a co-op that could change the brewing industry, an industry I'm in Asheville to cover, by the way."

He looked up, and she swore she saw relief cross his face. "That's it?"

"If it's anything else, it's really none of your business," she shot back. "Thank you for showing me the river." She turned and walked towards her car.

"I mean it, Alex. Be careful with him."

She stopped and turned to face him. "I'm always careful."

Chapter 15

Alex seethed. She got into her Outback and drove away, bare-ly refraining from squealing her tires. How dare he make any presumptions about her or her "connections." While there was no denying her physical attraction to the Riverkeeper, he threw up so many red flags she felt like she was surrounded by them. Besides, she didn't want to have the kind of long distance relationship Emily and Sergio were struggling with, and there was no way she'd leave Chicago. No, Max was definitely not her type. Especially since she wasn't even looking. After breaking up with her last boyfriend, she'd grown quite comfortable with being alone, and it would take someone pretty incredible for her to let anyone in.

Her thoughts turned to Roger. She knew their connection—be-cause Max was right that she'd felt one—was primarily due to his experience with breast cancer. It wasn't something she liked talking about and, in many ways, she'd had a lot of good things come out of the disease, but to be around someone who knew the constant dread of tests and wondering if it had gotten worse or better... Who knew the ritual of showing up at the cancer center, getting blood drawn, waiting for the pre-chemo meds to kick in, waiting for the lab to prepare the chemo, sitting in a chair for hours, knowing that the time right after that treatment would be the best she'd feel all week until the next one... How could there *not* be a connection?

Roger wouldn't personally know what that felt like, of course, but he would have seen his wife go through it. This was assuming he was an involved caretaker, which he seemed to be. He didn't wear a pink ribbon declaring he supported women with breast cancer, but he didn't need to.

Alex followed her GPS's directions through the mountains southeast of Asheville. She reached the address and stopped, staring at the driveway entrance. It looked like she'd be heading straight down the side of the hill. She eased her car over the lip and started descending, following the narrow asphalt strip through stands of evergreens and bamboo. The road began to ascend, and she reached a clearing filled with a huge brick house. The place had to be at least 10,000 square feet. A Harley stood in front of a massive portico that sheltered ten-foot double doors. She thought, briefly, of Max's admonition to be careful and wondered if meeting a stranger, alone, at his home in the mountains was a good idea. She checked her phone, surprised to see she had service, and shot off a quick text message to William.

I'm at Roger's. If you don't hear from me in an hour, grab Billy.
Do I have to wait to grab Billy?

Alex chuckled. *And come get me. You can see where I am?* Alex shared her location with William because she frequently traveled solo. It felt safer to know someone knew where she was, and William was the most mobile of her friends.

Sure can. You sure this is wise? Nevermind. Like you'd listen anyway. Be careful, and when you get back, I want to hear allll about your little boat trip with Mr. Hunky-Hunk.

Alex grabbed her bag with her notebook, ready to learn more about Roger and the plans he and Sergio had to keep Asheville's beer scene thriving. She raised her hand, but one of the doors opened before she had a chance to ring the doorbell.

"My system lets me know when someone enters my driveway," he answered her unspoken question. "Come on in."

"Doesn't that get triggered by wildlife? You seem to be pretty remote up here."

"It's got a weight threshold. About the only vehicle that could drive over it without setting it off is a scooter, and we don't get a lot of those up here."

Alex followed him through the house to the back. The layout reminded her of a mansion she'd seen in Door County, Wisconsin: they both had a center hallway with rooms branching off each side and a large kitchen in the back. Where the Wisconsin home had been high on a bluff overlooking Lake Michigan, Roger's place provided a spectacular view of the Blue Ridge Mountains. He gestured for her to head out to the deck, following with a tray containing a tea pot decorated with Chinese characters, a pair of fine porcelain cups, and a plate of biscotti. The juxtaposition of the large man carrying such a delicate display was incongruous, and Alex smiled.

"Didn't take me for a tea person, eh? Yeah, most don't. These were my wife's. She loved the whole tea ritual, and especially loved sharing it with guests." He shrugged. "I try to keep as many of the things she loved going."

He poured the hot beverage into both cups. Alex accepted the fragile vessel, pulling it to her lips. The steam warmed her face. The temperature had cooled the higher she got, and she was glad for the heat from the tea. "It's a lovely way to honor her," she said, then blew on the surface to cool it.

"The best way to honor her would've been to hold onto her brewery, but that didn't happen," he said bitterly.

Alex couldn't believe her luck. She wanted to learn about the co-op, but the most pressing matter was proving Sergio's innocence and that meant learning more about Mitchell and about Roger's past with him. She'd planned to steer the conversation in that direction, but hadn't known how, and here he was handing her an invitation out of the gate. "Losing it had to be hard," she murmured.

"You have no idea. It would have been fine if it had been to someone who actually cared about beer, the people, or anything besides the bottom line. But to Mitchell? That shark? All he cared about was money and power, and not necessarily in that order."

"I heard you'd known him a long time."

Roger grunted. "Oh yeah. We go way back. Grew up in the same little podunk town in South Carolina. Greg inherited a large fortune when his dad passed and wanted to see how quickly he could turn it into a small fortune. Didn't care how he did it or who he hurt, but I couldn't see that."

Alex waited silently, taking another sip of her tea, careful not to slurp.

"All I saw was dollar signs, you know?" His eyes focused in the distance, to some place long ago. "In high school I made the mistake of defending Greg against some of the guys on the football team. Poor runt followed me like a puppy dog after that. His dad died our senior year, and as soon as he got that money, he said he wanted to pay me back. I didn't think anything of it—we were kids, you know? He was going off to some Ivy League deal and I went the community college route. Then he left and I forgot all about his promise."

He stopped talking, lost in his past.

"You ended up in law school, right?"

He focused on her. "That's right; you were there when the bas–, I mean Greg threatened me and I brought up my legal experience. Yeah, I went to law school. Graduated and passed the bar and everything."

The lilting song of a cardinal caught Alex's ear; she saw a pair of the birds, a bright red male and a dun-colored female, dancing around a nest in one of the pines next to the deck. "How did you end up working with Greg?"

"Working *with* is being kind. I ended up working *for* him. He'd been gone about a decade. I followed his career, if you can call it that, out of sheer curiosity. Basically he made a living out of losing money. One failed venture after another. After his airline failed–why that man ever thought he could run an airline–he came back to our home town. I'd hung my shingle on Main Street, so to speak, handling any case that came my way, when he sauntered in. 'Looks like you've done pretty well for yourself,' he said. 'Want to do even better?' Of course I did. I was an idiot. I knew what he was like."

"Why do I get the feeling he cheated in school? Maybe even bought test answers?"

Roger laughed. "He sure did. Man didn't know an honest day's work if it bit him in his designer denim. He spent more on jeans than I spent on my whole wardrobe."

Alex swept her eyes over the extensive deck, the floor-to-ceiling windows, the outdoor furniture suite she knew cost a couple grand. The view alone was worth millions. "It seems like things have improved."

"They had," Roger grunted. "The craft beer scene had just started when he approached me, and he wanted a piece of it. For him, that didn't mean actually creating something. It meant finding out who was successful and buying them out. That's where I came in. I actually did know something about beer."

"Did you homebrew?"

"Sure did. I loved it. That's how I met Yasmine. We used to go to the same shop for supplies." Roger smiled wistfully. "This was the early 2000s, mind you. Brewing was a total bro-fest."

"In a lot of places, it still is."

"True, but it's getting better. Anyway, here's this petite, and I mean tiny woman coming in to buy beer making supplies and it was obvious from the get-go she knew exactly what she was talking about. I was hooked."

Alex studied his face. The stress that had covered it while he talked about Mitchell had disappeared. He looked more relaxed. Happy, even. He rattled his head to clear his thoughts, then leaned over to pour more tea. "I don't know what's gotten into me. You don't need to hear all this." He didn't speak for a few minutes, and Alex let him sit with his memories. "The long and short of it is, I helped Mitchell buy out all those breweries and made a ton of money doing it. Then I met Yasmine and I realized there were more important things."

"If you don't mind my asking, how did Mitchell get hold of Magnificat?"

"Medical bills. This?" he said, sweeping his arm to encompass his home. "Mortgaged to the hilt. She couldn't work, obviously, and I was a decent home brewer, but nothing compared to her.

Her disease progressed so quickly we didn't have time to train anyone to take over for her."

"Didn't she have an assistant?"

"Sure did. An assistant Greg was paying behind our backs. As soon as Yasmine was diagnosed, he saw it as an opportunity. He paid his little weasel to sabotage Magnificat. Suddenly we had supply shortages, staffing issues, you name it. I had no idea, of course. What happened at the brewery wasn't exactly important when my wife was dying. We needed money, and Greg pounced, just like he had when he showed up in my old law office, and offered the world."

Alex could picture it. And knew that assistance had come with a stiff price.

"Yasmine died, and at her funeral, Greg offered to help me out. Put some papers in front of me and I signed them. Me," he said, the anger flowing out of him, "an attorney. I signed papers and didn't even read them or know what they were. Signed my life away, again. Same song, different tune, but everything Yasmine had worked for was gone."

"I'm getting the feeling he wasn't well liked by anyone."

"Kinda hard to like someone who has no redeeming qualities. Literally none. The world's a better place without him. Leo's got his work cut out for him."

"Leo?"

"Detective Dunlap. He's good, but everybody and their brother and sister had a reason to kill Greg."

"The police seem to have focused on Sergio."

She could see that caught Roger by surprise. "Sergio? Damn. I didn't think he'd be their go-to suspect. I thought for sure Max would've been in their crosshairs."

Alex narrowed her eyes, thoughtful. "Because of Lisa?"

"Yeah," Roger nodded. "He adores that girl. And, as you might have noticed, he's got a bit of a temper."

"Unlike you."

He laughed. "Touché. But why Sergio? Seems kinda stupid to kill someone at your own fundraising event."

"Speaking of the fest, seemed like you and Mitchell had a major falling out. What happened, if you don't mind my asking."

Roger studied her for a moment before speaking. "I suppose not. It's not exactly a secret." He sipped his tea, the cup disappearing in his hands. "After the fog cleared, I realized what Mitchell had done. That he'd taken the brewery as payment for his loans. I lost it. Drove to his house and came this close to throttling the SOB."

"Understandable."

"But not very smart, and I'd already done enough stupid things to last me a while. No, I simply told him what I thought of him." Roger chuckled. "Now that was fun. I'm kind of going to miss making him pee his pants."

"He didn't..."

"Sure did. Worth the price of admission right there. But, his poor little pride was wounded and he called the cops. Tried to get a restraining order."

"Which didn't work."

"When you are universally loathed, the only way you get what you want is by bullying or bribing. Mitchell couldn't do either with our police." A look of satisfaction lingered on Roger's face.

Alex began to feel uncomfortable with his obvious pleasure at Mitchell's failure. She decided to switch subjects, hoping it would ease her tension. She tapped her phone so she could see the time.

"I've got to leave here in a little bit, but I did want to ask you about the co-op."

Roger's face brightened. "Oh man, this is going to be brilliant. See, Mitchell was able to buy up all those breweries because costs are so high, at least if you want to make decent beer. Working together, we can create economies of scale," he said, repeating what Sergio had said the day before.

"Why do I get the feeling this was your idea?"

He grinned, and she knew she'd nailed it. "I might have suggested it, but Sergio ran with it. Like he does. Give that man a kernel in the morning and he'll have a whole field of corn before sunset."

Alex's phone vibrated and the screen lit up. *Still alive or do I need to get on my horse and rescue you?*

She smiled. "Excuse me," she said, then tapped out a reply.

Alive and well. Leaving soon. What does Billy think of being called a horse?

He prefers stallion, thank you very much.

Alex replied with a crying-while-laughing emoji, then pushed her chair back and stood up. "That's my cue." Roger got up as well and she followed him through the house. When she reached the front porch, she turned and reached out her hand. He grasped it with both of his, and she felt a slight shudder course through her body. She ignored it. "Thanks for talking with me. And for sharing about your wife."

He squeezed her hand, then released it, a sad smile crossing his face and disappearing like a cloud that had briefly blocked the sun. "I don't get to talk about her often. People are afraid to bring her up. They think reminding me is going to be too hard. What they don't realize is there's no reminding necessary, because she's constantly in my thoughts."

Impulsively, Alex wrapped her arms around Roger, hugging him tight. "You can talk about her to me any time you want," she whispered.

The large man nodded. "Thank you," he murmured, then straightened up. "Well, you best get going before your friend decides you need to be rescued."

Alex looked at him, shocked. "How–?"

"Lawyer. I quickly learned to read upside down. Comes in real handy when you're across the table from your opponent. No worries, though. I get it. Attractive woman meeting a big man in his house in the woods? If I had a daughter, I'd tell her it's not a good idea."

Alex smiled, holding Roger's gaze. "But sometimes it is." She stepped off the porch, got in her car, and drove away, glad her need to focus on the steep, narrow driveway prevented her from watching him in her rearview mirror.

Chapter 16

Calliope checked a box on her clipboard, then picked up a bottle of Evan Williams, eyeing its contents. She set it back in its spot behind the bar and made another notation.

"Inventory, eh? That was my least favorite part of bartending."

The young woman turned away from her task. "You bartended?"

Alex nodded. "For years. It's how I put myself through school and how I paid the bills during my first several years at the paper. Journalism is not exactly the career to choose if you want a lavish lifestyle."

"Neither is brewing."

"Seems like some people do OK with it."

Calliope shrugged and continued jotting down the volumes remaining in the rows of bottles. "It's like all business, I suppose. Some do really well, others do fine, and a lot struggle to survive. Now that I think about it, that's life, too."

Alex's curiosity urged her to ask the young woman about her past, but her compassion kept her from doing so. If Calliope wanted to open up, she would. Humphrey jumped up on her lap and Alex grimaced as the cat's claws dug into her thighs. "What I don't get, and never have, is how it often seems like the worst of us are the ones who succeed."

"But do they, really?" Calliope set down her clipboard and leaned on the bar. "Look at Mitchell. The man had money, sure, but he was miserable. No friends, no respect. Not a single person liked him."

"Not even his wife?"

"Her least of all."

"Do you think she could have killed him?"

Calliope laughed ruefully. "Oh, absolutely I think she could have killed him. Do I think she did? No. Jackson told me Mitchell was drowned in his own beer, right?" Alex nodded. "There you go. Candy isn't that creative. Besides, she wouldn't take the chance she'd get any of it on her. It might ruin her fancy shoes."

Alex thought back to the suede boots Mitchell's widow had been wearing, playing with Humphrey's ear as she remembered. She would have noticed if the shoes had been stained with liquid, and they weren't.

"However," Calliope continued, "she could have *had* him killed. Now that I think about it, I wouldn't put it past her."

"What, like she hired a mercenary or something?"

Calliope's eyes swept the room, making sure none of the patrons could hear her, and leaned over to whisper. "Or convinced her lover."

Alex blinked. The idea seemed ludicrous, like something out of a bad movie, but when she was talking to Roger she'd had the same thought. She thought back to the interactions she'd seen at the festival the day before, drumming her fingers on the veneer-coated wood. "Vernon, huh?" she ventured, thinking of the man whose descent from respected brewer to Mitchell's lackey prompted her interest in Monolith in the first place.

"Got it in one."

"Do you know for sure they were, you know?"

Calliope shifted her gaze, focusing behind Alex. "Jackson, can you come here for a minute?" Alex turned to see the grinning young man, a reaction she assumed was due to Calliope's attention. He loped over and leaned on the bar next to Alex. Humphrey growled. Calliope frowned at the cat, but continued. "Want to tell Alex how we know Candy and Vernon were a bit more than friends?"

Jackson's face flushed bright red. He looked like he'd just had a hot flash, an experience Alex knew all too well. "Um, well, I..."

Calliope rolled her eyes. "Oh good grief. Fine, I'll tell her. Jackson here," she said, pointing her finger at the blushing man, "nearly walked in on those two."

Alex turned to him. Jackson gulped, his Adam's apple bobbing. "Nearly, meaning I didn't actually see them. But I, I sure did hear them."

"Jackson was delivering stuff about the festival to the breweries. He walked into Monolith, and—" she burst out laughing, then covered her mouth with her hand. The noise startled the cat, who jumped off Alex's lap, turned, and hissed. "Sorry, Humphrey, sorry. Anyway, the door was wide open but nobody's in the brewery, and then he hears..."

By this time, Jackson's color had returned to normal and he grinned at Calliope's mirth. "*Oh, Vernon, Oh, Candy*, etc. etc. It was pretty obvious what was going on." He giggled.

"Did they know you were there?" Alex asked.

"Nope. I just put the materials down on the bar and left."

"I'm surprised nobody saw you."

Jackson shrugged. "They weren't open yet. I was trying to get everything delivered early."

Vernon and Candy. That confirmed the rumors Max had heard, and definitely put a wrinkle in things. "Vernon seemed pretty upset about finding Mitchell like that," Alex said.

"If he 'found' him." Calliope looked at Jackson. "What do you think? You saw him. Did he seem genuinely distraught?"

"He did throw up."

"I throw up after killing someone, too." Alex raised her eyebrows, noticing the young woman's use of present tense. A slip, or nothing? Calliope hurriedly continued. "Not that I'd know anything about that. Not really." She glanced at Jackson again, a warning in her eyes. He raced around the bar and put his arms around her. She resisted, but then melted into him and began to cry silently, her shoulders shaking. A few minutes passed before she pulled herself away from her friend, grabbed a handful of bev naps, and wiped her face. She looked over Alex's shoulder and grimaced. Alex turned her head to see what had caused that expression and saw Sergio approaching.

"Alex Paige, I swear," he said, shaking his head. "I leave you alone with my people for a few minutes and you've got them bawling their eyes out. What'd you do?"

"She didn't do anything," Calliope murmured. "We were just talking about Vernon and Candy and Mitchell and how Vernon found him and—" Her voice hitched and she stopped.

Sergio stood next to Alex and reached his hands across the bar. He flicked his fingers and waited until Calliope stood across from him and grasped his hands. "Listen. I want you to take a break. Grab some water, go to the creek, and breathe. You're okay now, got it?" He waited until she looked up at him. "Got it?" he repeated. She finally nodded.

Alex watched the young woman as she filled a pint glass with water and started walking towards the door. Jackson moved to follow her, but Sergio stood to reach across the bar, tapped the young man on the arm, and shook his head. Jackson watched Calliope, the longing on his face so obvious Alex had to look away. She slumped back in her seat. "I'm sorry."

Sergio tilted his head at her. "For what?"

"I shouldn't have been talking about the murder, not to her."

"Why the hell not? You don't know what happened to her, and just because she's one of mine, doesn't mean you should tiptoe around her. Or him, for that matter." Sergio jabbed a thumb in Jackson's direction. "Nobody's life is all sunshine and unicorns. You know that better than anybody."

"Maybe not better than anybody," Alex said, smiling kindly at Sergio.

He waved it off. "It's not a competition. What I mean is, life is hard. It's how you react to it, how you deal with the BS, that decides whether you can live a happy life or if you become an evil SOB."

"Like Mitchell," Jackson muttered.

Sergio pointed his finger at him. "Exactly. Now there's a guy who had everything, right?"

Alex nodded. "Roger told me about Greg's silver spoon."

"You spoke to Roger?"

"Yes, this morning. I wanted to learn more about the co-op."

"And let me guess—somehow you started talking about the murder in an effort to clear my name."

"Maybe," Alex said, drawing the word out and plastering a sheepish look on her face. "Fine. I did. But he brought it up."

Sergio rolled his eyes with exasperation. "Alex Paige, please do not get involved. I know Leo—"

"That's Detective Dunlap, right?"

"Yep. He's a good guy, and a good cop. He'll figure this out."

"But what if he doesn't?"

"Leave it be, Alex. Remember what happened to Emily when you tried to catch a killer?"

Alex stopped protesting. She remembered all too clearly when a murderer held a knife at her friend's throat. But, she also knew she'd do anything to protect Sergio. She had to find out who killed Greg Mitchell to ensure Sergio wasn't falsely accused. She'd seen it happen before, and while Sergio was full of bluster, she knew underneath his tough facade, he was one of the most sensitive people she'd ever met. That was why he'd founded a non-profit to help Calliope and Jackson and others like them. Others like him.

Sergio shook his head. "I know that look. There's no talking you out of this, is there?"

"Nope. Absolutely not."

He sighed. "Fine. But stop going at it alone, OK? William brought an actual detective with him, so if you don't trust Leo, you could at least trust Billy."

Alex grinned. She'd been planning on working through everything with the couple anyway, and now she had Sergio's permission. Not that she needed it.

Sergio frowned. "You sly little minx. That's what you planned on all along, isn't it?"

"Who, me?"

He shook his head again. "Brat. You text William. I'll text Emily. If we're going to figure this out, let's do this together."

Alex lowered her head to her phone and tapped out a quick message, her hair hiding the grin on her face.

Chapter 17

William, followed closely by Billy, climbed the steps to the deck behind Alex's cabin. They'd decided to meet there so Sergio wouldn't be interrupted by his staff. Also, considering the subject matter, they didn't want any of his patrons to overhear them. Alex scooted her chair back to give the two men room, and William took the seat closest to her. "I wondered if you were ever going to text me. We've been bored to tears waiting for you to request our assistance."

Billy rolled his eyes. "Drama Queen." He pulled out the chair next to William. It was tight quarters, but all five of them managed to fit on the deck. Billy turned to Alex. "We were on the trails and wouldn't have gotten your text until we got back anyway. Good timing, by the way."

"I saw you brought your mountain bikes," Alex responded. Humphrey jumped onto the bench next to her. She reached over to pet him. He immediately began purring so loudly it was like somebody'd started a chainsaw. "I can't believe this love bug was a stray."

"That's what the attention of a good man will do for you," Emily said as she turned her chair around and straddled it. She'd walked up behind William and Billy, ending a call as she reached the top step.

"Everything OK?" Alex asked.

"Yeah. I just had to check in and let my sous chef know I wouldn't be back for a couple days."

Sergio grabbed Emily's hand. "You know you don't have to stay. Not with this crack A-team here."

"Yes, I do, and I don't want to hear another word about it."

Sergio raised his hands in surrender. "Yes, ma'am."

Alex went inside the cabin, shooing Humphrey so he wouldn't follow her, and returned with a tray of glasses and two pitchers, one filled with water and the other with beer. She set it down and began distributing the glasses while Sergio poured the beer. "One of the benefits of running a brewpub," he said, "is getting to taste the wares." He sniffed the beverage. "Is this Jackson's?"

"Yeah. That's his Helles."

"I didn't realize it was ready yet. It's unlike him to let others taste his beers before I've had a chance."

Alex winked. "I'm that charming."

"And don't we know it!" William called. The friends laughed and he raised his glass. "Let's get this party started, shall we?"

Emily frowned. "If this is your idea of a party, then skip me when you're sending out invitations."

"Yeah. Sorry. I get excited at the idea of putting the bad guys–"

"Or gals," Billy interrupted.

"Yes, or gals, in the clinker." William pulled his notebook out of the backpack he always carried with him and opened to a blank page. Across the top he wrote Who, Me, Mo, and Op, then drew lines to create columns.

Sergio leaned over the table, narrowing his eyes at the grid William had created, then spoke to Alex. "So this is what you two do. I'm pretty sure my name was on one of these."

Alex colored ever so slightly. "Well, you have to admit, you do come across as kinda dangerous."

"What, this teddy bear?" Emily teased.

"Teddy bear?" William scoffed. "I distinctly remember you thought he was a bully, and a thug, and a–"

Emily reached over and shushed William with a finger to his lips. She smiled sweetly at Sergio. "Absolutely. I thought he was a real jerk."

"Yes, well, I thought you were a grade A..." he paused and grinned, "chef."

"Nice save," Alex said.

Billy took the notebook and inspected the grid. "Let me guess. *Who* is your suspect. *Me* is Means, *Mo* is Motive, and *Op* is Opportunity."

William batted his eyelashes. "Bingo, spaghettio! This is why I love you."

"I highly doubt it's for *that* reason," Emily said under her breath.

"Let's just say it's one of many, many reasons. Anyway, enough fooling around. First: our suspects. Who hated Mitchell enough to want him dead? Besides everyone."

Alex cleared her throat. "I hate to say this, but let's start with the obvious. Sergio."

Sergio twisted his head to her. "What? You seriously think I could have killed him?" Anger and betrayal tore through his voice.

"No, of course not," Alex protested, then began enumerating reasons on her fingers. "But one, you do have a contentious, I mean *did* have a contentious relationship with the man. Two, he was bent on destroying a community you're passionate about. Three, he's rude to your people. Four, he's contributing to the pollution of the river. Five, you've got some sort of history with his wife." Sergio growled.

"Six, Mitchell was a jerk," William added.

"And finally, you're in Detective Dunlap's and Sato's sights, so we *have* to rule you out. That's the whole point of this exercise. We figure out who *didn't* do it."

"Ergo, the person left is the one who did."

Billy observed the exchange, leaning back in his chair with his arms crossed. "Fascinating."

"What is?" Sergio growled. "How they've all but pinned a murder on me?"

The cop shook his head. "No. Because they haven't. It's interesting to see how these two work together."

"So you approve?" William asked.

Billy shook his head. "I wouldn't say I approve. I would say I'm fascinated." He uncrossed his arms to grab his beer from the table. After taking a drink, he motioned for them to continue. "Please, don't let me stop you."

William scowled, then turned his attention to his notebook and began writing down names. "Let's see. We've got Max. He totally hated Mitchell, and why wouldn't he? Then Jackson and Calliope."

"What? Not those two. They're just kids," Sergio protested.

Emily put her hand on his arm. "They're in their twenties. I know you're protective of them, but this should help protect them."

"Should?"

"Once Ms. Marple and Mr. Poirot over here figure out Calliope and Jackson didn't have either means or opportunity, because we know they had motive," Sergio growled, but Emily kept going, "because *everyone* had motive, then we'll know they didn't do it and they're off the list."

"May I continue?" William asked, his pen poised over the next blank line.

"Don't forget Candy and Vernon," Alex suggested.

"Why those two?" Billy asked.

"They were having an affair."

"They were *what?*" Sergio blurted, genuinely surprised.

Billy nodded. "Makes sense."

"Why's that?" Alex asked. She could tell he'd noticed something. When she and William had met Billy after someone was murdered in Door County, they'd quickly learned that the detective was fair, thorough, and very, very observant. Since then, William had discovered a whole lot more about him.

"Just something I noticed."

"Typical. Tight-lipped. You know you're not on the clock right now," William complained.

"Once a cop, always a cop. And this is a murder, so whether I'm on their clock or not, I can't turn it off."

"Or won't. Which is excellent for us and our dear friend. Right, Sergio?" William grinned at the scowling chef.

"Fine. Add Roger, too."

William flicked his eyes at Alex. "Why Roger? I mean, beyond the confrontation we witnessed."

"Because Mitchell basically stole his wife's brewery out from under him after she died," Alex said softly. The four of them focused on her. Even the cat stopped cleaning himself. Thinking about someone who'd died from the same disease she'd survived always caused Alex to pause. *That could have been me*, she thought.

"But it wasn't you." Emily knew her so well she knew exactly what Alex was thinking. Her friend spoke gently and with so much compassion that a tear escaped. She wiped it and squeezed her friend's hand.

"What a bastard," Billy said, surprising them all. "What? I'm still human."

"You're one of the kindest people I know," William assured his partner, then turned to Alex. "I take it you learned about this from Roger?"

She nodded, then filled them in on their conversation.

"So Roger's definitely got motive," William said, checking the column.

"Why do you even have that column?" Sergio asked, somewhat scornfully. "They've all got motive; that's why they're on the list or else you wouldn't include them."

Alex responded. "Not always. There have been times we knew someone had the opportunity, but couldn't figure out the motive."

"Like that last one," William said, reaching across to squeeze Alex's hand. She shuddered. "He was a piece of work."

"How many murders have you two, ahem, investigated?" Sergio asked.

"Too many." Alex stared off into the forest, remembering not only the people who'd died in the last few years, but also the seemingly countless deaths she'd covered during her time as a reporter. Except they weren't countless. She remembered every one.

Emily gently cleared her throat. "In this case, I guess you can check everyone's box for motive."

William nodded, then did just that. "Since our first order of business is to clear Sergio's name, let's start with him."

"Great."

"Do you want us to help or not?"

"Fine. But let's get it over with, OK?"

"Let's see. Mitchell was murdered by someone drowning him in his own beer. Poetic, I'll give them that."

"Was he tied down?" Emily asked. "I couldn't see with all those people in the trailer."

Billy nodded. "He was strapped to the recliner with nylon rope."

They all looked at Sergio. Alex remembered they'd used nylon to create barriers all around the festival.

"Seriously?" Sergio asked. "I thought you were supposed to be ruling me out, not tying the noose."

"Patience, oh gruff one. Patience." William tapped the notebook with his pen. "So maybe someone was trying to set you up. Was this a two birds with one murder situation? Know anyone who'd want you out of the picture, too?"

Sergio shook his head. He opened his mouth to answer, then stopped abruptly. Alex turned to see what had caught his attention. Detectives Dunlap and Sato were approaching the deck.

"Sorry to interrupt your little shindig, Sergio," Sato said. He stood on the stairs and looked down at William's notebook. William quickly turned it over, but from the frown the detective gave him and then Billy, it was obvious he'd seen what was on the page. He shook his head, then focused on Sergio again. "We're going to need you to come with us."

Sergio leaned back. "Am I under arrest?"

Dunlap and Sato exchanged a glance. "No. We just have a few questions."

William rolled his eyes. "That is so clichéd. Seriously. 'We just have a few questions.' Straight outta every bad cop show out there."

Sergio glared at William. "You're not helping matters."

"Didn't you already ask all your questions?" Emily asked through clenched teeth. Alex had her hand ready in case she needed to prevent her friend from pouncing on the detectives.

"More evidence–" Dunlap began.

"Has come to light," William finished. He stretched to look around Dunlap. "Nope. No script. You must have your lines memorized."

"William," Billy said so quietly Alex barely heard him.

William sat back with a huff. Sergio stood up. "Let's get this over with." He scooted around Emily, who had already pulled out her phone. Alex assumed she was calling Sergio's lawyer. He nodded at her, then kissed her on top of her head. "I won't be gone long."

"We'll be right behind you," Alex said to him.

Sergio smiled sadly. "I know." He turned to Dunlap. "What station? So Emily can tell Ethan where to meet me."

"I'm sure an attorney won't be necessary," Sato growled.

"When dealing with the police, an attorney is always necessary. Where are you taking me?"

Dunlap glared at his partner, then told them the station. Emily repeated the information into the phone, then hung up. "Ethan will probably beat you there," she said, then stood up. She gripped Sergio's hand and turned him around. Her eyes focused like lasers on his. "We've got you. No matter what, we've got you, OK?"

As Sergio looked at Emily, Alex could see a tiny hint of fear in his eyes. After being unjustly accused of murder, and imprisoned, in his teens, he knew the system wasn't always fair.

Billy eyed the two detectives. "You sure about this, Leo?"

"Would we drive all the way out here if we weren't?" Sato snapped.

Dunlap sighed. "No, we're *not* sure," he said. "That's why we want to ask him questions and are not arresting him."

"Yet," Sato said.

Dunlap tilted his head back and looked at the trees above. "No, not yet. We have questions, that's all."

"Your partner sure seems to think otherwise," Emily said.

Dunlap stared at her, then looked at Alex, William, and Billy, settling on the fellow detective. "You helping this group?" Billy shrugged, but didn't say anything. "You should know better."

Billy held his gaze, keeping silent. Dunlap finally broke the stare and motioned for Sergio to lead the way. "I'm assuming you'll all be following me?"

None of them moved. Sato looked pointedly at the empty pitcher and the pint glasses on the table. "Might want to wait a while. I'd hate for anyone to get pulled over on the way to the station."

Sergio jerked his head towards the detective. "Are you seriously threatening them?"

Dunlap shook his head. "No, no he is not, are you, Detective Sato?"

Sato focused on Dunlap, pinching his lips together. "Let's get this over with." He turned on his heel and disappeared around the corner of the cabin. Dunlap motioned Sergio to walk in front of him, then followed without another word.

Emily stared at where they'd been standing. "This can't be happening."

"But it is," Billy said. "Let's go. I'll drive." He waited for William to get up, then pointed at the notebook. "Bring that."

"Yes, sir," William said. He waited for Billy to walk around him and gave Alex a tiny smirk. He turned to Emily. "We're not going to let them pin this on Sergio, you know."

Emily nodded. She stood ramrod straight. "I know."

Chapter 18

Billy hugged the curves tightly, maintaining a consistent distance behind the other SUV. They'd occasionally lose sight of the detectives' vehicle when the road bent, but they'd see it again as soon as they reached a straight section. William sat in the front passenger seat, slightly turned to face Alex and Emily in the back. He handed the notebook to Alex. "You take over. If I do it, I'll make a mess."

"Should you drive?" Emily asked.

"No," William and Billy said simultaneously. Billy glanced at Emily in the rearview mirror but didn't say anything. William faced forward and explained. "He's in cop mode. When he's in cop mode, he drives."

"What does that even mean?" Emily asked.

"It means he's focused and will be much better at keeping up with those fools than I am."

"They're not fools," Billy said tersely. "They're just doing their job."

"Sato certainly strikes me as foolish," William said, then glanced at Billy, whose lips had compressed to a thin line. "But you're right. They're just doing their job." William reached over and patted Billy's thigh, a move Alex was sure would annoy the detective.

Instead, Billy reached down and squeezed William's hand, his eyes focused on the road the entire time.

Alex opened the notebook. They hadn't gotten very far before the detectives had interrupted them. "Jackson's next. First, though, what time was Mitchell killed? We need to know that to figure out where everyone was."

"Some time between noon and one," Billy answered. "It looked like he went to his RV to have lunch."

"Alone?" Alex asked.

Billy shook his head slightly. "Maybe not. There were two place settings."

"Oooh—does that mean fingerprints?" William asked.

"No. They were never used."

Alex wiggled the pen back and forth, then flipped to a blank page and wrote *Timeline* at the top. "Do we know who was meeting him?"

"Wouldn't that be neat and tidy?" William answered.

"Sure would, but no, we don't." Billy slowed and followed Detectives Dunlap and Sato into the parking lot of the police station. Alex could see Ethan leaning against a Land Rover with his arms crossed. The lawyer must have left as soon as Emily had called him. Alex wasn't surprised. Sergio inspired that kind of loyalty. Billy parked, then turned to his three passengers. "I'll go talk to Ethan. You three continue your exercise. Maybe you'll have it figured out by the time I get back." He got out and closed the door. The three stared after him.

"I can't believe he's OK with this," Alex said. "He's so by-the-book."

William turned in his seat and shrugged, grinning. "He knows it won't do any good to fight it. I might be a wee bit—"

"Stubborn?" Emily teased.

"Charming. I'm a wee bit charming. He can't resist me when I set my mind to something. Obviously," he said, wiggling his eyebrows.

Emily rolled her eyes, but she grinned back at him.

"Alright you two, let's get this timeline figured out. Somebody joined Mitchell in his RV between noon and one. I'm thinking closer to noon."

"Why's that?" Emily asked.

"The way he was killed. They had to tie him down and then drown him," Alex explained.

William nodded. "Billy told me it looked like the killer took his time."

"Or her," Emily said.

"Sorry. Yes. His or her time. But I'm leaning towards a man."

"Because he was tied down?"

William nodded. "Wouldn't you need someone strong, maybe physically intimidating, to get Mitchell to let himself be strapped to a chair?"

"Not if they had a gun pointed at him, or a knife" Alex said.

"Good point." William drummed his fingers on his chin. He stretched, then grimaced. "I need to move. There's a picnic table right over there. Shall we?" He exited the car without waiting for an answer. The three regrouped at the table, which was set in a small park next to the station. "Alrighty then. So, the fest opens at eleven, and by one Mitchell is dead. Or, at least that's when Vernon 'found' him." William used air quotes around the word *found*.

"You really think Vernon could have done it?" Emily asked.

"I think all of them could have done it. Except Sergio, of course. And Calliope. Although..."

"What are you thinking?" Alex asked him.

"She did mention something about 'when she kills someone.'"

"Don't you dare," Emily spat. "That, that right there, that nonsense is why Sergio started The Onion Squad, because people make assumptions and judge them. They can't get a fair break, can't ever be seen for who they are because of something that happened in their past."

At first a look of anger crossed William's face, but then he lowered his eyes and sighed. "You're right. You're so right. I'm sorry."

"We do have to be objective, though," Alex said softly.

Emily bristled, but then relaxed. "I know. I just want these kids to have a decent chance. They've been through so much, and to be judged all the time... it's so hard on them."

"How's Sergio holding up?"

Emily shrugged. "He's putting on a brave face, but that's Sergio. The Masked Man. Keeps everything shoved inside."

"That way no one can hurt him," William said.

Emily nodded. "The fact that he's opened up to me as much as he has—which isn't much, mind you—has been surprising." She looked up and a smile crossed her face. "Speak of the devil."

Alex followed Emily's stare to see Sergio exit the station. He looked around, then saw the group at the picnic table and walked over. Ethan and Billy followed closely behind him. William moved closer to Alex to make room for Billy, but Sergio didn't sit. Instead, he paced back and forth. Emily patted the bench next to her, but he shook his head. "Can't. Not yet." He walked away from them towards a small creek. There were creeks everywhere in Asheville, Alex thought incongruously. Sergio clenched his fists, then picked up a rock and threw it across the water. It struck a tree on the other side, the sound so loud it reverberated like thunder. They all watched him, silent until Ethan spoke.

"It's not looking good," the lawyer said.

"You know he didn't do this," Emily protested.

"Of course I do. But there are a lot of things pointing to Sergio. The rope, for one."

"Anybody can get rope," Emily scoffed.

"Yes, but it was his fest and he knew where the rope was stored. Then there's the minor detail of their major confrontation."

"Mitchell confronted everyone he saw," William said.

"Did everyone threaten him?" Ethan asked.

They all paused to think. "Roger did," Alex volunteered, reluctantly. "And so did Max. He said he'd kill him."

Ethan waited for other responses. None came. "Did any of you see Sergio between noon and one?" he asked.

Emily seethed. "I thought you were his friend. What, is he not paying you enough?"

Ethan glared at her. "I've known Sergio much, much longer than you, Ms. Kincaid. Don't you dare malign my relationship with him. We've been through more together than you'll ever know." He took a deep breath, his eyes focused on Sergio, who still stood at the creek with his back to them. "I'll ask again, because if any of you did see him during that time frame, that's his get out of jail free card."

"Probably not a great phrase to use," William said, eyeing Emily.

Ethan ignored him. "Sato is focused solely on Sergio. Dunlap is not. However, he has to follow the evidence."

"If I may?" Billy ventured. When Ethan nodded, he continued. "There doesn't seem to be much, or any, physical evidence beyond the ropes. They said they're checking for DNA?"

"They *what?*" Emily exclaimed.

Billy put his hand up. "But you know how inconclusive evidence like that can be. Of course Sergio handled the rope. It's his fest, right? He was in charge."

William eyed Billy appreciatively. "And how did you get this info, pray tell?"

Billy shrugged. "One cop to another."

Ethan chuckled. "Don't let him fool you. This one's a master at getting information. I tell you, I wouldn't want him to question any of my clients. He baited Sato until he blurted out what they had."

"And it's enough to be worried?" Alex asked.

"No, it's not." They turned to see Sergio walking towards them. "My DNA is probably on some rope that I gave out to several people working the fest. That, and the fact that I hated Mitchell, are the only things they've got."

"Then why is Ethan here worried?" Emily asked.

"Because not only did he have a very public chest-beating with Mitchell less than an hour before he was murdered, but also because of his past," Ethan answered. Sergio glowered, but the lawyer continued. "Sato is convinced. 'Once you kill someone, you'll do it again.' He actually said that."

"It was self-defense," Emily said hotly. "AND, it was decades ago".

"I know that," Ethan replied, "so do all of you, and so, fortunately, does Detective Dunlap. But Leo can't give Sergio any slack or Sato will be all over it."

"This sucks," William said.

"Agreed." Ethan pointed at the notebook in front of Alex. "Normally I'd advise against becoming involved and just let the pros handle it, but Sergio?" Sergio looked at his friend. "For some reason, Sato wants to nail you for this. I'll do what I can, but if you all can point the finger somewhere else, it'll help. We just need reasonable doubt."

"I thought we needed that in court," Alex said.

"We need it now, to prevent this from going to court." Ethan walked around the table and grasped Sergio's hand. "You are not going to have to deal with that. You are not going to be arrested. Too many people are counting on you." The lawyer held his friend's gaze until Sergio nodded. "I've got to run, but Billy, keep me in the loop."

Billy nodded. Sergio came around the table and stood next to Emily, but didn't sit down. She looked up at him, got up, and the two walked to Alex's car. The rest glanced at each other before silently following.

Chapter 19

Calliope prowled back and forth behind the bar, glancing up when Alex entered. She didn't stop prowling until she saw Sergio, who trailed his friends. She ran towards him and plowed into him, practically knocking him over.

"Whoa, whoa. I'm okay," Sergio said, laughing.

"Jackson told me you'd been arrested," she said, glaring at the young man who was cleaning off a table.

Jackson looked up. "That's what I heard. One of the other guys saw you shoved into the back of a cop car and the rest of you tearing out behind them."

"First of all, I wasn't shoved, and secondly, they did not 'tear out' after us. They just wanted to ask me some questions. That's all."

Calliope searched his face, then relaxed slightly. "I was so worried. What if... I'm sorry. If I'd known they'd come after you..."

Alex considered her. What was she apologizing for? "What would you have done? If you'd known Sergio was the primary suspect?"

The bartender swallowed, glancing at all of them in turn before settling on Sergio. "I... I saw Vernon talking to Candy next to the trailer. It looked like they were fighting." Alex noticed Calliope wasn't looking Sergio in the eyes.

Sergio studied her. "When was this, and why weren't you at our tent?"

"Um, I had to go to the bathroom. I think it was around noon. Maybe earlier?"

William and Alex looked at each other. "Are you thinking what I'm thinking?" he asked.

"Maybe. It's a possibility. Calliope, are you sure it was noon?"

She barely raised her shoulders. "I think so? I don't really know, but it seems about right."

"It was closer to 11:30," Jackson called, smiling shyly.

Of course he would know, Alex thought. Ever since she'd met Jackson she'd observed that any time he was around Calliope he couldn't take his eyes off of her.

"How long were you gone?" Billy asked, his voice matter-of-fact. William eyed him.

"Um, I don't know. Maybe ten minutes?"

"It was twenty-five," Jackson corrected. "We started to get really busy and it seemed like you were gone a long time."

Calliope glared at him. "There was a long line. What, I'm not allowed to go to the bathroom?"

"Relax," Sergio said. "I'm sure that's not what he's saying at all."

Alex sought William's eyes again. If Calliope was back before noon, then both she and Jackson had alibis. "Was anyone else working the tent with you?"

"Yeah. Roger jumped in to help. He happened to be nearby when Calliope had to go." Jackson blushed slightly.

"How long did he stay?" Alex asked.

"I dunno. At least forty-five minutes. I think?"

Alex relaxed. That gave Roger an alibi, too. She'd been worried he wouldn't have one, but it wasn't until he was cleared that she realized how much that concern had affected her.

"Sergio, do you remember what you were doing between noon and one?" Billy asked, his tone casual.

Sergio shook his head. "Probably putting out fires. It's all a blur."

"Of course it is. It was your first festival. I'm still pissed you had to shut it all down because somebody decided to do the world a favor."

"Emily..."

She hung her head. "I know, I know. But there isn't a single person who's going to miss him."

They stood silently as they all considered how sad it was for a person to be murdered and have no one to mourn him.

"Can we get back to the whole Candy and Vernon sighting?" William asked. "That, to me, seems rife with possibilities."

Just then a large group entered the brewpub. Calliope returned to her spot behind the bar and Jackson greeted them, then led them to a large table. Alex was surprised they wanted to sit inside until she glanced out the window and saw rain falling. Sergio watched the group, then swept his eyes over his friends. "Guys, I appreciate what you're doing. I really do. But I need a break." He looked at Emily. "I just need to be alone for a little bit."

She nodded, squeezed his hand, and watched him as he headed towards his office. Emily sighed. "We have to clear him."

A couple entered the bar. "It's starting to get crowded in here," Billy said. "Not surprising. People have probably heard what happened and need to fulfill their morbid curiosity."

"And we need to figure out who did this," William said. "Your place?" he asked Alex. She nodded and they all ran across the clearing to her cabin.

Hours later, William and Billy headed back to Bessie and drove her to their campsite. Alex was exhausted. She was also frustrated. William had worked himself up into a froth, convincing himself and nearly all of them that Candy had talked Vernon into killing Mitchell. "The only thing tying them to this is Calliope's word that she saw them," Billy kept reminding him.

Billy had a good point. Alex had a disturbing feeling that she didn't want to probe. If Vernon was in cahoots with Candy, as William put it, they were going to have to find some solid proof if they wanted to clear Sergio's name, and Sato definitely had it out for Sergio. Alex had seen that kind of focus before, and it never ended well for the recipient.

"Do you think they did it?" Emily asked her. She sat curled up in a recliner, wrapped in a comforter and holding a cup of tea. She'd skipped the Donkey mug this time and chose one of the more standard ceramic cups hiding in the back of the cupboard.

Alex inhaled lemongrass and ginger from her own cup, guaranteed to soothe her wobbly stomach. Or so she hoped. She felt so inadequate, like she was missing something that was right in front of her and if she didn't figure it out, and soon, her friend would be arrested. And she was afraid Emily would never forgive her, even though she knew that was a ridiculous thought. "I don't know," she sighed. "I don't think so. Vernon—well, I just don't believe he could do it. The way he reacted…"

Emily grimaced. "Yeah. That was pretty gross."

"But I wonder about Candy–" A knock on the door interrupted Alex. She got up from the couch to see who it was. "Come in, Sergio. You doing better?"

He stamped his feet, then snapped his umbrella open and closed to shake off the rain. He left it on the covered porch, then crossed to Emily and took her hand. "I figured I'd find you here."

She gave him a small, tender smile. He helped her up and she led him to the couch. "Trade you places?" she asked Alex, who nodded and moved over to the recliner.

"Hey Sergio," Alex began after she got settled. "I need to ask you something that might be a little awkward."

He fell into the couch and put an arm around Emily when she sat down next to him. "I've fielded awkward questions all day. Go for it."

"What's the story with you and Candy?"

"Story?"

"Don't be coy," Emily said, leaning away so she could look at him. "It's obvious, and was even more obvious the last time I was here, that you two have some sort of past. I didn't ask then..."

"Why now?"

"We're exploring possibilities, including finding out who'd want to frame you," Alex explained.

Sergio chuckled. "Exploring possibilities," he repeated. "C'mon, Alex. It's me. No need to beat around the bush. In fact, I insist you don't." He pulled his arm from around Emily's shoulders and leaned forward, directing his intense gaze at Alex.

"Fine then. Somebody wants to pin you for murder. Candy and Vernon are our most likely suspects right now–"

"Candy and Vernon?"

Alex waved her hand, frustrated at the interruption. "Yes, Candy and Vernon. William is convinced that Candy talked Vernon into killing Mitchell."

Sergio stared off in the distance, then shook his head. "Candy's a lot of things, but I don't see her doing that."

"Which brings me back to my original question: what's the story between you two?"

Sergio paused. He glanced at Emily, who sat in the corner of the couch with her arms crossed. She didn't say anything; just returned his gaze. "We met in juvie," he began. Emily's eyes widened slightly, but she stayed silent. "She'd been there about a year when I arrived. Really knew the ropes. She was one of the few people who was nice to me when I got there."

"Why was she there?" Alex asked. Emily continued to stare at Sergio.

"Theft. Some vandalism." He stopped, lost in his memories.

"Care to elaborate?"

"No."

"I know you feel like you're breaking a confidence, but this will stay between us. We just have to figure out what's going on."

Sergio sighed. "She's fought so hard to get beyond that. You saw her. Would you guess she'd been arrested multiple times?"

"Yes," Alex and Emily said simultaneously.

"You might have some blinders on," Emily said. Alex didn't detect any bitterness in her friend's tone. More like resignation.

"Maybe. Maybe so. Like I said, she was nice to me. Few people were.

"Anyway, I guess she began with petty theft. You know, candy bars at the convenience store, makeup at the drug store. It was thrilling, she told me, knowing she could get away with it. All they saw was this cute little innocent-looking blonde thing, she'd say."

"Until they didn't, right?" Alex asked.

"I think she could have gotten away with it forever, but she wanted more. Began recruiting her other little friends. They set up a whole ring of cute, innocent-looking thieves. They'd give the goods to Candy and she'd sell them to their classmates, at a steep, steep discount." Sergio snickered. "Little devil was only 13 when she got caught."

Emily narrowed her eyes. "You sound like you admire her."

Sergio shrugged. "No, I don't. It's sad. She had it all; loving parents, big house on the hill–literally. They had this gorgeous view. But it wasn't enough. I knew what that was like; everything looked great on the outside. Except she really did have loving parents."

"Not like you," Alex said softly.

"Mom was. Mom was loving." Sergio stared at the floor.

"Sergio," Alex started, pulling him back to the present, "Do you realize what you just told us?" He looked up at her, then at Emily. "You just told us Candy's good at getting people to do what she wants."

"She's a real Tom Sawyer," Emily said, then stood up and began pacing. "What happened with her last time I was here?"

"It was nothing," Sergio said. "She calls me every now and then to complain about something in her life. Tells me I'm the only one who'll understand, since we came from the same place."

"Except you didn't," Alex said. "You were there because you were protecting yourself. She was there because she committed crimes."

"And brought others down with her," Emily accused. "How many of her little cronies ended up in juvie because of her?"

"None," Sergio answered. "I know you don't think much of her–" Emily scoffed "—but she didn't point the finger at anyone. She took full responsibility. She only told me about it because she felt like we bonded."

"And did you?"

"Em, there's nothing between Candy and me. She just wants someone to talk to who won't judge her."

"They have therapists for that. And how many years has it been? It's been decades, Sergio."

He sighed, but didn't say anything.

"I think we have to consider that William may be right," Alex said. Sergio shook his head vigorously, but she raised her hand to stop him before he could defend Candy. "We have to look at the reality. She hated her husband and was having an affair with someone who also hated him."

"And I'm betting when the will's read, she'll get it all."

"But why would she want to pin it on me, if that's what you're thinking?"

Emily rolled her eyes. "Because she knows your history, Sergio. She knows the cops are going to look at someone like you first. That's why you've done all this," she said, sweeping her arm around the cabin, "to keep others from looking at Jackson and Calliope the way they looked at you." She sighed. "Sometimes you're too blind.

Sergio glared at her, then walked to the door. "Candy did not decide to kill Mitchell and get Vernon to do it, and you cannot convince me otherwise." He opened the door, grabbed his umbrella, and stomped off into the rain.

Chapter 20

Alex focused on the open door. Fresh air floated into the cabin, causing the candles she'd lit to flicker and bringing the earthy scent of moss inside. She shivered from the cool breeze left in Sergio's wake.

Emily stared at the door. "Fool. He's a damn fool." She turned to face Alex and slumped her shoulders. "Should I go after him? I should go after him."

Alex shook her head, walked to the door, and closed it. "Maybe give him a few."

Emily nodded. "Probably a good idea. Let him realize I'm not the enemy."

"No, you're not, but you know how protective he is of people he cares about."

"What I don't get is why he'd care about her. She's manipulative, whiny, and spoiled."

"But do you think she's capable of murder?"

"Yes. I do, and so do you." Emily walked over to the recliner to grab her phone off the table next to it. "I'm going back to my cabin. Whether he's ready to see me or not, I've got to check in with my staff and see how things are going. Besides our annual Fall break, I've never been away for this long, not since we opened."

Alex wanted to hug Emily, but could tell her friend didn't want the gesture. "I'm sure things are fine, but I understand. I'm going to see what I can find out about Candy and Vernon."

"And Max?" Emily asked, studying her friend's face.

"Max? Oh, yeah. I should probably look into Max, too."

"I know you don't want to believe he could kill someone," Emily said softly.

"That's precisely the problem," Alex said. "I do believe it."

Alex's phone buzzed and she rolled over to check the screen. "Ugh," she moaned. It was two in the morning. Emily had sent her a text message. *He's still not back.*

He's probably at the restaurant.

Exactly where I should be. At my own, I mean.

Everything OK?

No. I've got to head back in the morning.

It is morning.

:-P No, seriously. I've booked a flight. Alderman Idiot is on the rampage.

Alex frowned. The Alderman for the ward where Elements was located was not happy when Emily expanded her restaurant. He'd wanted to put a fast food chain owned by a celebrity in the spot. Emily fought him and won, but he hounded her. She was constantly bombarded with threats and inspections.

What a jerk.

I have a few stronger names for him. Favor?

Sure. Anything.

If Sergio gets over his temper tantrum and I'm gone, tell him where I went?

Of course. You don't want to tell him?

Nope. He wants to storm off, he can storm off.

Alex shook her head. Emily had no patience for, as she called them, temper tantrums. Alex also had a suspicion her friend was pulling away because she was getting too close to the temperamental chef. She chuckled to herself. They were both temperamental chefs. Alex was surprised it had taken this long for the two to have a spat.

Got it. Need a ride to the airport?

Nope. Uber. Butt crack of dawn.

Keep me posted?

Always. And ditto.

Alex signed off with a heart emoji. She stared up at the ceiling, a night light providing a soft glow. She understood Emily's frustration, but she could also see Sergio's struggle. He truly wanted to see the best in people, even if they were, as Emily put it, manipulative, whiny, and spoiled.

Sleep eluded her. Thoughts of Max forced their way into her consciousness. More like images, as she remembered the Riverkeeper from their excursion on the French Broad. She could almost feel the muscles of his back as they bunched and released. Alex blew out a frustrated sigh. Not only didn't she have time for this, she also had no desire to get involved with the bad boy type. She'd gotten that out of her system years ago. At least, she thought she had.

She swung her legs off the bed, finally giving up on sleep, and padded over to the breakfast bar to open her laptop. After Emily had left, Alex had dug into newspaper archives to see what she could discover about Candy and Vernon. It turned out that Candy's past wasn't a secret after all; in fact, she'd turned herself into a media darling. Poor little rich girl who reformed after being shown the error of her ways. She'd rebranded herself as a do-gooder. Alex mentally slapped her own hand at the thought. She knew people could change. Had seen it over and over. But Candy? Alex wasn't buying it.

All the publicity stopped when Greg Mitchell entered the picture. Alex found their engagement announcement, and then the clips of their wedding. It had been a short engagement. Alex bet Candy probably thought she'd hit the jackpot and could continue her rise as one of Asheville's most sought-after philanthropists, but that's not what happened. After the wedding announcement, the name Candy—or Candace, because she'd begun using her full name during her transformation—never appeared in print again. Every single time she was mentioned, it was as Mrs. Gregory Mitchell.

Alex bristled. This habitual subsuming of women into the men they married had always made researching their pasts challenging. It also made her angry. Any time she wrote about a woman, Alex used her first and last names, never dismissing who she was as a person.

Candy and Greg had been married for over twenty years. That was a long time for a person who sought the limelight to be hidden in the shadow of another. That could have been what had drawn Candy and Vernon together. The brewer also practically disappeared once he entered Mitchell's world. Gone were the frequent profiles and accolades in magazines, newspapers, and trade publications. He didn't even merit a mention in the press release announcing Monolith Brewing, and he had the barest of bios on the brewery's website. He'd been under Mitchell's thumb for about a tenth of the time Candy had, but it certainly gave them something in common.

Emily's comment about Max was what had gotten Alex out of bed, so she opened her favorite source for newspaper archives and plugged in his name, then sorted by oldest result first.

Alex rocked in her chair, glad the bar stool had a back so she didn't topple over. An image of a clean-cut Maximilian Xavier Wells, class of 1991, beamed at her. She couldn't help herself from smiling back.

He was even handsome as a teenager, grinning at the camera like he didn't have a care in the world. The newspaper had run a profile on the state's high school cross-country champion. Max hugged a large trophy with one arm and a young girl with the other. Even in the faded black and white print, Alex could see her adoration and figured it must be Lisa. The caption confirmed it.

Alex continued searching. She didn't expect to find any smoking guns. However, this process of learning as much as she could about a subject helped her form a more well-rounded picture. She did it with places, and she did it with people. Her ability to dig up the past had helped put away criminals, including murderers.

Would Max be one of them? She hoped not, but she'd seen evidence of his temper multiple times, and she could tell he'd do anything to protect his sister.

Max appeared in her search results fairly frequently. His athletic prowess put him on the front page of the sports section a few times. He'd moved from cross-country to wrestling to mixed martial arts, and had excelled in each sport. She leaned back, thinking. The more she learned about him, the less likely she thought it was that he'd killed Mitchell. With his physical abilities and his temper, Alex didn't see him being so patient as to drown someone a pint at a time. No, she imagined Max would have taken a much more direct approach.

Alex yawned, stretching her arms over her head. She wondered how long Sergio had known Max, but did not look forward to asking him. He'd know immediately she was looking at the River-keeper as a suspect and he'd be mighty unhappy with her. Maybe she could ask Max? Yes. It would be better to talk directly with him anyway. Things hadn't ended so well during their last excursion. She'd extend an olive branch. Alex checked the Riverkeeping website and clicked on the *Do Your Part* link. The page listed upcoming dates for volunteering, and she noticed an opening to help clean a section of the French Broad the next morning. "Perfect," she said to herself, then registered for the 8:00am slot. She groaned. That was going to come awfully early, although she knew she'd be up at dawn no matter how many hours she was awake in the middle of the night. She wished she could ask William to join her, but knew if she texted him about anything that early, he may never speak to her again.

Although she really wanted to go back to bed, now that she knew she'd be seeing Max the next morning she continued her search. Through the stories on the screen, Alex watched him age. She found the announcement of his appointment as Riverkeeper. He'd also authored many pieces, penning several articles about his passion. Over the months and years his tone became increasingly strident, and when she got to an editorial criticizing his tech-niques, accusing him of vandalizing businesses along the river and insisting he be arrested, she wasn't surprised. She was even less surprised to see the signature at the bottom of the angry missive: Gregory E. Mitchell, Esquire.

"Esquire?" Alex said to the empty cabin. "What a pompous...Who uses Esquire any more?"

She yawned and stretched again, then stood up, realizing if she didn't get to bed, she'd fall asleep on her computer. Alex stopped in the bathroom and studied her own face. She looked as tired as she felt. "One of these days," she said to her reflection, "you're going to have an easy trip. No drama. No dead bodies. Just a nice, easy trip. Right?"

She didn't wait for a response. She knew she wouldn't like the answer.

Chapter 21

"Alex! What are you doing here?" Roger's deep voice boomed from the vehicle next to hers. She stepped onto the gravel and smiled as he got out and walked around the front of his truck.

"Probably the same thing you're doing," she replied, then searched the small group of people milling about next to the parking lot.

"He's not here. Max, I mean. I presume that's who you'd hoped to see."

Alex turned back to Roger and smiled. "Well, sure, I figured he'd be here, but it's great to see you."

Roger grinned, then extended an arm to her. "May I have the honor of escorting you to our assigned duties?"

Alex laughed and wrapped her hand around his bicep. It felt wonderful to laugh, and she realized it had been days since she'd responded to anything with pure pleasure. Learning that Roger was helping Jackson and Calliope when Mitchell was killed had been an immense relief. That was three people she could rule out, and Sergio was one more, although she still needed to establish Sergio's whereabouts.

That left Candy and Vernon, who were possibly in cahoots together, even though Alex hated to think the brewer could be a murderer. And then there was Max.

If she were going to be totally honest with herself, she hated that idea even more.

"Hey Roger." a spindly man with shaggy hair approached them. He wore a bright yellow vest that looked like it would glow in the dark. "You must be Alex Paige," he said, stuffing his clipboard between his elbow and waist. He reached out a gloved hand.

Alex released Roger and shook the volunteer's hand. "Toby?" she said, reading his name tag. "Pleasure to meet you."

Toby handed her and Roger each a pair of plastic gloves and a trash bag. "Alright everyone. We're all here now. Most of you know the routine. We'll split up into two groups. One goes that way, and the other goes the other way. We'll go about a mile and there'll be someone waiting at either end to bring everybody back." He divided the volunteers. Alex was glad that she and Roger would be with Toby. She figured if he was leading one of their clean-up efforts, he'd probably know Max pretty well.

The trio picked their way through the undergrowth, keeping their eyes on the ground and looking for trash. Alex was appalled. Everywhere she looked, she saw bottle caps, crushed cans, rumpled chips wrappers, and other detritus.

"This is awful," she said. "Who would just throw their trash out here?"

"It's despicable," Toby said fiercely. "Some of it is accidental. People float down the river and something falls overboard, or wind picks things up from overflowing bins." He bent over to grab an empty 12-pack box, then shook it at her. "This, however, this is intentional."

"And it's only gotten worse since Monolith took over Magnificat," Roger said.

Toby nodded in agreement. "People who drink there, they don't care. They buy their crappy beer, go down to the river, and just dump their trash."

Roger grunted. "What they should be dumping is what's inside them."

Alex picked up a fast food bag overflowing with empty wrappers and stuffed it in her garbage bag. A french fry box fell out, and she bent back down to retrieve it. "How long have you been doing this?" she asked Toby.

"Years. I saw one of Max's articles and looked him up. I grew up around here and it was nice to see somebody who finally gave a damn." He stopped at the edge of the water. They were no buildings, factories, or houses around. As they stood in silence, watching the river flow, it was like they were the only three people in the world.

Alex broke the silence. "Were you at the festival Saturday?" she asked quietly. To speak any louder would have been to break the spell cast by the idyllic scene. Idyllic, except for the bits of garbage she could see extending along the French Broad's banks.

Toby shook his head. "No, but I heard what happened." He cleared his throat. "We better get a move on or the others'll beat us."

Roger chuckled. "They've got a little competition going. Whoever's back last buys the beers."

"I take it you've volunteered before?" Alex asked.

"Frequently. Seeing you isn't just dumb luck. I'm here almost every week."

"Sometimes twice a week," Toby added without turning around.

"I heard you jumped in to help Jackson when Calliope had to leave for a bit. That was nice of you." A sparkle caught Alex's eye and she plucked a silver bracelet from the mud.

"That's why I was there. To help out whenever somebody needed me."

"You seem protective of Jackson," Alex said, then turned to look at him

Roger stopped, a question on his face, and then it cleared. "Oh, because Mitchell pushed him. I just can't stand bullies."

Alex laughed. "You can't—couldn't stand Mitchell."

"This is true."

They walked for a few yards without encountering any more garbage, to Alex's relief. She was beginning to understand why Max was so angry all the time. How people could ruin a place of such natural beauty through sheer laziness was something she'd never understand.

"Well, it was still a nice thing to do." They continued in silence until Alex said something that had been on her mind. "I'm curious about something," she began. "Why did you stop practicing law?"

Roger snorted. "Because I felt like that's exactly what I was doing—practicing. After signing my life away to Greg, I realized I obviously wasn't very good at it."

"That's not being very fair to yourself. You were focused on Yasmine."

"I appreciate you trying to put a positive spin on it, Alex, but I was an idiot and a fool. I told you, I knew what he was like. I'd worked for the man and helped him destroy businesses just like my wife's, and yet I trusted him anyway. I thought he was sincere, that there was no way he'd screw me over. That maybe somewhere inside him was an iota of good." The big man stooped under an overhanging branch and picked up a stray bottle cap while he was bent over. He straightened, then continued following Toby. "Like I said: I was an idiot."

"It's not a bad thing to believe people can change."

Toby barked out a laugh, but didn't turn around. "You obviously never met Greg Mitchell."

"Briefly."

"That should've been enough." Toby picked up the pace. "C'mon. We want to beat those guys. I am not paying for beers today."

They followed him in silence for a few minutes, then Alex spoke up again. "What about Candy?"

"What about her?" Roger asked, eyeing her from the side.

Alex shrugged. She wanted to watch Roger's reaction, but she needed to focus on her feet lest she trip on one of the exposed rocks or roots. "I know she had a difficult past, but it seemed like she was trying to make up for it, and then she spent twenty years with someone like Mitchell. I don't get it."

Roger grunted. "You are the PollyAnna type, aren't you."

"That's what William always says."

"Well, Mrs. Candace Mitchell would do anything—and I mean anything—to get what she wants. For years, that meant being married to Greg. Until it didn't."

Alex stopped. "Are you saying...?"

"Make of it what you will," Roger said without stopping or turning around.

They continued walking. Alex could see a clearing up ahead. Through the trees, Max waited for them. The Riverkeeper smiled at Toby, but the greeting on his face disappeared as soon as he saw Roger. When he realized Alex was the third in the team of volunteers, he scowled, turned to the van, and got in without a word.

Alex rolled her eyes. *This is why I'm single*, she thought. *And men say women have mood swings*. Toby grabbed their nearly-full trash bags and put them in the back of the vehicle, then he and Roger piled in, leaving the front seat for Alex. She swung in, buckled up, and turned to Max. "Well, this is a pleasant surprise."

"I see you found a lot of garbage," he said. Alex didn't think he was referring to the litter they'd picked up.

"Sure did," she said brightly, ignoring his implication. "This must be a never-ending job."

Max didn't respond, just pulled out of the lot, spitting gravel as he went. They sped to the meeting point and Toby let out a whoop as another van pulled in right behind them. "Yahoo! Beer's on them!"

"Seems like somebody could use a few," Roger muttered.

Max's lips thinned. He turned off the ignition and got out without a word. Alex stared after him, then turned to the back seat. Toby shrugged, then opened his door and followed the River-keeper.

Alex raced to catch up. She pulled alongside Max. "I was hoping to see you."

"I thought you were with Roger," he growled.

Alex rolled her eyes. "No. Seeing him was a surprise. But thanks for the assumption. Actually, I signed up because I wanted to talk to you."

"So that's why you volunteered?" he said with a sneer.

"Yes, frankly. But I'm also glad I did. *And* I'm also glad I did. Seeing all that trash... I can see why you get so angry."

Max gave her a sideways glance. "It's a never-ending job."

The two stood a short distance from the group of returned volunteers. There was a lot of good-natured kidding along the lines of who was slow, who cheated, and who was buying the beers. They also compared how much trash they'd cleaned up, putting a somber note on things.

"Can I ask you something?" Alex began. When Max glanced at her, she continued. "What's up with you and Roger? It seems like you abhor him."

The Riverkeeper focused on her. "I do. Do you really want to know why?"

"Yes."

"Are you sure? Because it seems like you two have–"

"A connection?" Alex cut him off. "Of course we do. I had breast cancer. His wife died of breast cancer. Do I really need to say 'Duh,' or is it obvious enough that's what I'm thinking?"

Max laughed, surprising her. "Fair enough. I have a habit of making assumptions."

"So I'm gathering." Alex watched Roger laughing and kidding around with Toby and the others. Even though he appeared to be relaxed, there was tension about him, like he was holding something in. Was it just grief, she wondered, or was it something else? "What is it about him that you don't like?"

"Oh, there are lots of reasons, but mainly it's because he's one of the most unethical people I've ever met, besides Mitchell. Fitting that those two worked together for years. The damage they did, the lives they ruined... I'll never understand what Yasmine saw in him."

Alex eyed him. "You knew Yasmine?"

"Yeah, but it's not like we hung out or anything. Sergio and I would pop into Magnificat now and then. She always seemed nice. Normal. Like she really cared about people."

"Was Roger different then?"

Max narrowed his eyes. "Maybe. I didn't pay a whole lot of attention to him."

Alex didn't believe him. There was something deeper between the two and not just a butting of heads because of their different philosophies. She kept those thoughts to herself. "Do Roger and Candy have a history?"

Max barked. "I thought you were a travel writer, not a romance author."

Alex bristled. "Are you always such a jerk?"

He paused, considering. "Most of the time? Yes," he said, surprising her. "But to answer your first question, no. From what I've seen, Roger has always hated her, and the feeling's mutual. Why do you ask?"

"Just a feeling," she shrugged.

"You've obviously decided I didn't kill Mitchell," Max stated bluntly.

"Because I'm asking you about the other players?" When he nodded, she explained. "You were never near Mitchell's tent during the festival, so you couldn't have done it."

"Ah, checking up on me, are you?"

Alex turned to face him. "You, and everyone else who had a reason to commit murder. It's too bad you have an alibi."

"Why's that?" Max looked bemused, which was infuriating.

"Because, of everyone involved, you have the biggest motive. And, I might add, the worst temper."

Max looked at the crowd of volunteers, who'd begun climbing into the vans. Toby waved them over. "C'mon," he urged. "It's time these slackers ponied up."

"Yes, sir," Max responded, then focused on Alex. "Wrong on both counts," he said, then walked away.

Chapter 22

The room hummed with conversation. It wasn't the normal timbre of friends enjoying each others' company. It was fraught with tension and anger. Alex paused at the threshold, almost reluctant to interrupt whatever was causing such negative energy. She felt William approach before he rested his chin on her shoulder. "What's going on here?" he murmured. Alex turned to him and shrugged. Billy stood behind him.

Sergio looked up from his spot behind the bar, then motioned them in. They sat across from him and he passed a piece of paper over the varnished wood. Alex scanned it. The letter, signed by Candace Mitchell, was on embossed letterhead with "Cease and Desist - Antitrust Violations and Unfair Trade Practices" as the subject line. It went on to describe how the formation of the Bee City Brewers Cooperative would cause the potential for "market dominance, price fixing, and exclusionary practices." Alex gave the notice to William, who snorted. "Hypocrite much?" he said, passing the paper to Billy.

"A cease and desist letter? Really?" Alex asked. Sergio nodded, his face a mask. "You don't seem surprised."

"Nothing that woman does surprises me."

Alex swiveled her barstool so she could scan the room. She recognized several of the people who'd been working at the festival on Saturday and realized they were all brewery owners. "Did everyone get one?"

"We sure did, that low-down conniving piece of–" The woman who'd served Alex the basil bitter at the festival, who'd been so excited about the possibility of the co-op, practically spat. "Wouldn't surprise me in the slightest if she'd killed Mitchell. Bet this was her plan all along."

The group assented. "You got that right, Jody," one of them said.

The door to the brewpub opened and Roger walked in, then stopped at the entrance just as Alex had. "What are *you* doing here?" Jody growled. The rest of the brewers grunted.

"Not a good idea to show your face after this," one of the men said, shaking his copy of the letter.

"Well, this could get interesting," William muttered.

Roger flicked his eyes to him, then stared at Alex before brushing his eyes over the room. He put his hands in his back pockets and took a deep breath. "I get it. I understand why you're mad."

"Do you?" the same man yelled, getting out of his chair so abruptly he knocked it over. "We trusted you. You told us you knew Mitchell, and you knew Candy, and she'd back off now that he was gone."

"What can I say? She's a woman. I can't help it if she changed her mind."

Alex stared at him in shock. This was not the man who'd spent time cleaning up the river with her that morning, or the one who confided his pain about the loss of his wife. Or was it? she considered. She barely knew him. All of it could be an act. A very good act, but an act nonetheless.

Every woman in the place, and there were several, as well as many of the men glared at the big man. "Are you really that stupid?" Jody seethed.

Sergio laughed. "Wow, Roger. You sure do like taking your life into your own hands. Don't come running to me when they tear you apart."

Alex picked up the letter and read it again. Candace Mitchell had sent the formal notice. Roger's name was nowhere to be found. "Did you have something to do with this?" she asked.

"No. I told you I don't practice law any more."

"But you know what it is."

"Of course. Sergio emailed me a copy and asked me to join you all."

The room collectively focused on Sergio. He came around from behind the bar to stand next to Roger. Before he could explain, Jody spoke up. "I know you believe in second chances, Sergio, but this is too much," she said. The rest of the brewers agreed.

"Now hold on, just a minute," Sergio said. "Roger's got a past, but don't we all?"

"Not like his," one of the brewers muttered.

"He's also apparently a misogynist," said another.

"Apparently?" William scoffed. "I'd say he's a card-carrying member of the He-Man Woman-Haters club."

"No wonder he and Mitchell got along so well," Jody sneered.

Roger rolled his eyes. "I was being facetious, you idiots."

Alex could feel the entire room bristle. She crossed her arms and leaned back against the bar, studying Roger. She remembered snippets of conversation with him over the past few days: his surprise that a tiny woman could be into brewing and the way he spoke to Alex when she discovered his wife had died of breast cancer. At the time she'd felt comforted, but looking back, it felt condescending. "There, there," he'd said, like she'd skinned her knee at recess and wanted someone to kiss her boo-boo. Alex wondered if underneath his facade as a grieving widower and someone who wanted to make up for his past was still the man who would help a bully like Mitchell destroy lives. She considered Sergio, who stood next to the big man. Would her friend be that blind to Roger's faults, she wondered? How far did his belief in redemption go?

She scanned the room, registering that Vernon was sitting in the back. Roger must have noticed him at the same time, because he spoke again, directing his attention to Monolith's brewer. "I'm surprised to see you here, Vernon."

"Leave him alone," Jody snapped.

"Why? If you think I'm a pariah, he's even worse."

"Worse? Are you nuts?" shouted the man who'd knocked over his chair. It still lay on its back. The angry man strode towards the front of the room, towards Roger. "You're the one who sold out. You're the one who let that snake in. Vernon didn't have a choice."

Roger advanced on the man, looming over him. "You think I did?" he said, jabbing his finger into his sternum. "My wife was dying, you asshole. I would have signed my own death warrant if somebody'd put it in front of me."

The room went silent, so quiet Alex could hear the gulp of the brewer who'd accused Roger.

Roger stormed to the closest table and snatched one of the letters. "This is nothing. I may not have been a great lawyer–"

"You can say that again," Jody muttered.

"But even I know this is a bunch of legalese. They have nothing to stand on. I also reviewed your articles of incorporation. At

Sergio's request," he explained when several people protested. "Everything looks good, and now that Mitchell's out of the way, you've got nothing stopping you. You're welcome, by the way."

Alex gasped. William gripped her hand. "Is he saying..."

"Shhh," Alex admonished him, but it was too late. Roger shifted his attention to the two friends at the bar.

"You people really do think I'm an idiot, don't you? No, I am not saying I killed Mitchell. Did I want to? Of course I did. We all did. Including, maybe especially, Vernon. Can you imagine what it must have been like to work for that man? Because I can, and if that doesn't make someone want to kill him, they're a better man than I am."

"Finally, you said something that rings true," Jody said.

"That I killed Greg?" Vernon squeaked. "I didn't. I swear."

She rolled her eyes. "No, you fool. That you're a better man than Roger. Of course, that's not saying much."

Roger laughed. "Good one, Jody." He turned his attention back to Vernon. "Everyone knows about your little fling with Candy." Most of the crowd gasped and swiveled their heads towards Vernon. They erupted with murmurs of *What?* and *No way!* "Oops. I guess they didn't know. Now they do."

Vernon's face flushed deep red. Alex could feel his rage from across the room. "So what?" he spat. "She was miserable. He–he made her life miserable."

"What happened, Vernon? She convince you to take care of him, once and for all?"

"What? No! Candy would never do that. She was going to leave him," Vernon protested.

Roger belted out a deep-throated laugh. "Sure. Sure she was." He wiped the mirth off his face. "Do you really think that gold digger would leave her cushy set-up for a broke brewer who lost everything?"

"Sure you're not talking about yourself, Roger?" Jody asked.

Roger directed his steely gaze to the stout woman. "Positive. She's not my type." He shifted his focus to Alex. "I prefer my women to be less artificial."

Alex returned his gaze and didn't look away. She kept her face as impassive as possible, not willing to let anyone in that room see what she suspected. Roger finally turned back to Vernon, and his face softened. "When did she first bring it up? Killing Greg, that is?"

Alex thought maybe he wasn't as terrible a lawyer as he claimed, because his interrogation techniques were spot on.

Vernon blanched. "I didn't kill him."

"But she wanted you to, didn't she?"

He stared at Roger, then lowered his eyes to the floor. "Maybe. She kept saying how much better life would be if Greg weren't around, that somebody should do something about him."

"So you did."

Vernon snapped his head up. He looked around the room, a pleading look on his face. "No," he said firmly, while shaking his head. "No, I didn't."

"No, he didn't," Jody affirmed. The room shifted its focus to her. "He couldn't have. He was with me when somebody put Mitchell out of his misery."

There was a collective gasp. "Oh really," Roger said suggestively. "Seems like Vernon here's quite the ladies man."

Jody guffawed. "That's rich, Roger. I needed help changing a keg—"

"What, too heavy for you?"

"Pig. I had a long line, saw Vernon walking by and asked him to change it. He did, then stuck around to help me pour."

"What time was this?" Billy asked. It was the first time he'd spoken since they entered Layers and Alex had practically forgotten he was there.

"11:45," Jody answered without hesitation. "He stuck around 'til about 12:40, when he got a call and said he had to go."

"You seem pretty certain about that," Roger said.

Jody scowled at him. "Because one of my interns—now former interns—was supposed to be there at 11:30. I had to man the tent by myself. Vernon got there just in time."

"Seems like Vernon has an alibi," the man who'd knocked over his chair said. "Kind of hard to be in two places at once."

"But you found the body, am I right?" Roger asked.

Vernon simply nodded.

"And several of us saw the aftermath of that," Billy said. He spoke directly to Vernon. "That's an awful experience. If you want to talk to somebody, I can help you find someone."

William wrapped his arm around Billy. "And this is why I love you."

"So who does that leave?" someone asked. "Does this mean Candy killed him?" asked another. The room looked at Roger, who smiled briefly, then shrugged.

"She had more reason to want him dead than anyone else." He held up the letter all the brewers had received. "Especially now that we know she plans to continue his legacy."

"What about Sergio?" a man wearing a flannel shirt asked. "No offense, but I heard they've been questioning you."

"It's under control," Sergio said.

"How? Sato hates you," Jody said.

"Sato hates everybody."

"And you hated Mitchell," said the man in flannel.

"And so did you," Sergio replied. "All of us did, and for good reason, but none of us are killers."

"Except you did kill someone."

Sergio focused on the man. He didn't respond to the allegation. He didn't need to, because Jody turned her full energy on the accuser. "Stuff it, Nate. You know better."

Nate shrugged. "Just pointing out the obvious."

"So what would happen if you got arrested?" another brewer asked.

"One, I'm not going to be arrested, and two," Sergio said, pointing his thumb at Roger, "he's got everything in order for the co-op." Several of the people in the room erupted in anger. "Stop. Stop right there," Sergio boomed, loud enough to be heard over their protestations. "Roger is a much better attorney than he claims, and he knows the industry. Even more importantly, he's intimately aware of the tactics used by Mitchell and, apparently, by Candy. He's the best person to handle this."

"I don't trust him," Jody said, glaring at the big man.

Alex agreed. She wished she could pin down what had changed her perception of Roger. She wished Emily were there so she could hash things out with her. William was great, but like Alex, he also saw the best in people. Emily was a bit more cynical, or as she liked to call it, realistic. Emily had been put off by Roger from the start, and even though she hadn't said anything to Alex, she knew her friend's radar was pinging.

William leaned in. "I can feel your spidey senses. What's up?"

Alex shook her head, keeping her focus on Sergio and Roger. "Later. I think I have a plan."

Chapter 23

Sergio's phone rang. He pulled it out of his back pocket and frowned at the screen. "What's up?" he said when he answered the call. His face clouded with anger. "How long?" He nodded while he waited for the reply. "OK. Thanks, man. And thank Leo for me, too." Sergio hung up, put the phone in his back pocket, and spoke to the room. "Sorry, folks, but something's come up and I've gotta head out. Jody, can you make sure everyone gets out and lock up for me?"

"Sure thing."

"Thanks." He walked over and gave her a set of keys, then walked to the bar. He approached Alex, William, and Billy and spoke under his breath. "That was Ethan. Apparently Sato's on his way here right now to arrest me."

William jumped off his barstool. "Then we need to leave right now."

"I'd recommend waiting," Billy said.

"Why, because leaving will make me look guilty?" Sergio scoffed. "He's already decided I'm guilty. Whether I stay and wait for him to slap the cuffs on me or not won't matter."

"Now would be a good time for you to remember you're off the clock," William said to Billy.

Billy scowled at him, but nodded slightly. "Fine. Alex, you said you had a plan."

"Yes, I do. But we need to get out of here." She stood up. "Roger," she called. He looked up and began making his way towards her through the string of brewers exiting the building. "Did you drive your truck or your Harley?"

"Truck. Why?"

"We're going to need it."

***

Alex circled the island in Roger's kitchen, mentally going through the plan they'd hashed out on the way to his house. She'd wanted Roger to drive so there wouldn't be a bunch of vehicles in his driveway. As she made another lap, she vaguely registered the fresh flowers in a glass vase that sat in the center of the granite, although she did intentionally pinpoint the location of the knife block. Just in case. "Just in case," she muttered. "I'm a travel writer. This is ridiculous."

Sergio entered the room, followed closely by Roger. "Are they in place?" she asked. Roger nodded.

"I don't like this," Sergio said. "I don't like this one bit."

"I know. I also know if anything happens to you, Emily will never speak to me again."

"Same holds true for you. You sure about this?" he asked, searching her face.

Alex flicked her eyes to Roger. "Yes. No. Maybe." She shook off her doubts, which were mostly centered on the big man. She was taking a huge gamble that this time her instincts were right.

Roger opened a drawer and pulled out a roll of twine. "I guess this'll do." He focused on Sergio. "You ready?"

Sergio rolled his head on his shoulders. "No. But that doesn't matter, does it?"

The trio crossed into the combined living and dining room. Roger pulled a chair from the table and dragged it in front of the fireplace. A bell chimed. The television above the mantel came to life and they watched as a black Mercedes entered Roger's driveway. "We've got about five minutes before she gets here," he said. Sergio sat in the chair and Roger began wrapping the twine around his ankles.

"Ouch, man, not that tight."

"I have to make it look real."

"But do you have to make it look *that* real?"

"Who knew big tough Sergio was such a baby?" Roger finished tying Sergio's legs to the chair, then pulled his arms behind him and wrapped the twine around his wrists. Alex could see the binding squeezing his flesh.

"It definitely looks like you mean it," she said.

"What are you still doing in here?" Roger glanced at her with annoyance. "Get in the pantry before she gets here and sees you."

Alex took one last look at Sergio's bound figure, then followed Roger's instructions. She opened the pantry, its slatted door facing the fireplace. She heard another bell, and turned just enough to glimpse the shine of headlights on the windows before closing herself in. Alex could see Sergio through the cracks, but barely. He was struggling against the tightness of his bindings. She willed herself to calm down. She checked, for at least the fifth time, that her phone was set on silent, then opened her recording app. Before she could press the red circle, a text appeared on her screen.

Everything in place?

Yes. You? she replied.

Good to go. You sure about this?

No. Glad Billy's here, though.

You and me both.

Roger opened the front door before the bell rang. Candy entered, then stood on her tiptoes to kiss him on the cheek. "I'm so glad you called. I knew it was only a matter of time," she purred. He pulled back and turned Candy to face the living room, holding her at arm's length.

"I brought you a present," he said into her ear.

Candy's eyes opened wide in shock, and then she cackled—actually cackled, Alex thought—with glee. "Oh Roger, you should have, you definitely should have." She sauntered towards Sergio, slightly dragging her suede boots on the carpet as she made her way towards the bound man. She dragged a fingernail across his chin. Sergio ignored her, clenching his jaw and staring straight ahead. Candy looked up at Roger and crossed her arms, jutting her hip out. "To what do I owe the pleasure?"

"They got your little letter," Roger said, eyeing her. "I told you not to send it yet."

Alex slapped her hand over her mouth to keep from gasping. Sergio's eyes shifted briefly to the pantry door, then focused again on the big man. She wondered what Roger was doing. He knew this was all being recorded; he knew the plan.

"I couldn't wait any longer," Candy pouted.

Roger sighed. "Your impulsiveness may have been charming when you were younger. Now it's just dangerous. Do you know where I was tonight?"

"How would I know that?"

"I was at Layers, trying to calm down a bunch of whiny brewers all up in arms because you couldn't wait a few more days. I had to take matters into my own hands," Roger said, pointing at Sergio, "or they'd be rallying behind this one. Without him, the whole co-op idea goes bye-bye."

"You're a fool," Candy said, her voice still sultry. "A big, dumb, enormous fool. We didn't have to wait a few more days."

"And why not?"

"Because Sato was on his way to arrest Sergio before you decided to kidnap him. Good lord, Roger. I knew you were stupid, but I didn't think you were *that* stupid." Candy walked lazily to the dining room table, turned a chair around to face the living room, sat down, and crossed her legs. She swung her calf up and down, then straightened her legs and leaned forward. Alex stifled another gasp. Candy's blouse had stretched across her back and revealed the outline of a gun. Alex frantically tapped out a text message.

She's got a gun.

WTF? Where'd she hide it?

WHO CARES? Sergio can't get loose. Please tell me you and Billy are in place.

Sorry. Right. We are. Ready when you are.

Hold on. I'll let you know.

Alex watched through the slats, anxiety tearing at her. She could see Sergio trying to work his arms free. At least Roger didn't use zip ties, she thought. When he'd suggested it, Alex said absolutely not. She'd had a bad experience with the constraints and wasn't about to put her friend through that.

Roger glanced at the pantry door. Alex wanted to scream at both of them to stop looking her way. Candy was too feral; she'd notice it if they didn't stop. The big man walked to the fireplace, flipping a switch to turn it on. Flames leapt from the fake logs. Sergio tried hopping his chair to get away from the heat, but Roger put his hand on the back to stop him. "Candy here is convinced you killed her husband. She's so convinced she got Detective Sato to believe it, too."

Sergio's eyes widened slightly. "So that's why. I knew he hated me, but I didn't think he hated me that much."

Candy leaned back in her chair again. "It's less about hating you than wanting something else. Poor man actually believes I'm interested in him."

"Apparently so does this poor man," Sergio said, tipping his head towards Roger. Roger smacked him, hard enough to nearly cause the chair to fall over. Alex hoped he was just a good actor and that she hadn't made a huge mistake.

"Oh, I'm interested in Roger, alright." Candy stood up, her movements languid, but Alex could see how taut the muscles in her forearms were. "I'm interested in his questionable moral character. Greg certainly got a lot of use out of it. Now it's my turn." She reached behind her back and pulled the gun out of her waistband, pointing it at Roger.

"Candy, what are you doing?" he said, surprisingly calm.

She sneered. "Taking care of business. Just like I did with Greg. You wouldn't, despite everything he'd done to you, and that coward Vernon wouldn't hurt a bee if you gave him a million dollars. I offered him even more, and he still wouldn't take care of that rotten SOB."

"You," Roger said, like he was dumbfounded. "You killed him. You killed your husband?"

"Did I? I think Sergio did. Yes, Sergio murdered my beloved Gregory E. Mitchell, Esquire. He told me to seduce Greg, convince him to let me tie him up so we could play a widdle game, since he was such a naughty boy." She sauntered over to Sergio and caressed his cheek. Alex practically growled from her hiding place, but she didn't dare move. "And then Sergio, my big strong man, came in and drowned that bastard in his own swill. So poetic." She laughed, a hideous sound that echoed around the room. "At least, that's what dear Detective Sato thinks."

Roger still looked dumbfounded, even though they'd all agreed on the way from Layers that this would probably be her story. Maybe he really was that good of an actor. Alex sure hoped so.

"So what happens, Candy?" Roger asked softly. "You kill Sergio, then kill me, then act like you were caught in the middle?"

"Now see? You're not as dumb as I thought you were. Poor little me, loved by two violent, violent men." Candy moved, switching her aim to Sergio's head.

NOW NOW NOW Alex texted to William. A bell chimed and Alex cursed. *Roger was supposed to turn off the alarm for the back door. Why didn't he?* she thought. Candy yanked her head to focus on the pantry. She pointed the gun towards the slats.

"Come on out. Now," she commanded.

Alex swallowed. She set her phone on a shelf, confirming it was still recording, then slowly opened the door and edged along the wall towards the kitchen.

"Stop right there. I should have known you'd be here. Nosy little b—."

"Don't you call her that!" Roger shouted, cutting her off.

"Oh yes, that's right. We've got our little cancer club here, don't we?"

Alex couldn't believe the magnitude of this woman's evil. "What are you going to do, Candace, kill all of us?"

She shrugged. "Why not? Roger, be a dear and get some more of that twine. On second thought, Alex, you fetch it. You do anything I don't like and Sergio here gets it."

Alex glared at the woman, hearing William's voice in her head. She knew he'd be scoffing at Candy. "Who says gets it?" he would have laughed. But he wasn't there, not yet. Alex backed into the kitchen, eyeing the knife block.

"Un unh," Candy said, waving the gun. She was leaning back to see Alex in the kitchen. "Just the twine. And hurry up."

Candy turned back to face Roger and Sergio while Alex walked to the end of the cabinets. She mimicked rummaging through the doors. "It's in the island," Roger said, "remember?"

Alex pivoted, then walked to the island. She loudly opened and closed several drawers, trying to buy time.

"What's taking so long? Get back in here now or I shoot off a toe." Candy glanced over her shoulder, but her body faced Sergio.

Alex put her hands on the granite to steady herself. Candy didn't see her as a threat, just as they'd hoped. Alex closed her eyes, then inhaled deeply. When she opened them, she reached for the heavy crystal vase. She thought about dumping the flowers, but they were roses. Roses with thorns. "Found it," she called, making sure her voice was shaky. She walked as silently as she could towards the living area. Candy still had her back to the kitchen. *This is what you get for bring arrogant*, Alex thought, then she hurled the vase towards the woman. The cut glass vessel slammed into Candy's back, causing her arm to swing wide. Roger leapt towards Candy, grabbing her wrist and forcing her to drop the gun. The front door banged open and Detective Sato burst through.

From behind, a hand shoved Alex aside and she fell into the pantry door, breaking slats as she pounded into it. Officer Brooks ran past her, followed closely by Billy and William with Officer Ortiz in the rear. Brooks grabbed Candy's wrists, yanked them behind her, and slapped zip ties on them. *Now* she *deserves zip ties*, Alex thought.

Detective Sato stood in the entryway, his gun pointing at Sergio. His eyes swept the room, landing on Candy. He put his gun back in its holster, then strode across the room to stand over her. "Fancy meeting you here."

"Izzy!" she cried. "Look what they've done to me!" Candy twisted her body to display her bound hands.

Detective Sato stood motionless, except for a slight twitch at the corner of his mouth. "I thought you liked those kind of games."

She blinked rapidly. "Only with you."

"Candace Mitchell, you have the right—"

"Izzy," she pleaded, tears forming. "This is all a big mistake. These two murdered Greg. They're trying to frame me."

Detective Sato laughed. "You're a piece of work. And the name's Isaiah. *Izzy*," he mocked. "Glad I'll never have to hear that again."

"But you said you loved me!" Candy wailed.

The detective gave her a wicked smile. "Words are cheap. Just like you."

Roger opened a switchblade to cut the twine binding Sergio to the chair. Sergio rubbed his wrists. "Seriously, man. What'd I ever do to hurt you?" Roger reached out his hand to help Sergio up, and the two gave each other a man-hug with lots of backslapping.

"Told you. I had to sell it. And she bought every bit of it."

Alex tried to open the pantry door, but her fall had wedged it tight. William came over to help and the two forced it open. She reached in, grabbed her phone and stopped the recording. She pressed play. "I'm so glad you called. I knew it was only a matter of time," Candy's voice purred.

Epilogue

A man in a canoe floated in the middle of the river. A group of people in inner tubes floated towards him, calling out numbers. They butted up against him and he reached into his Igloo, pulling out several packages and handing them across. The group waved and drifted away, following the river's pull.

"Are those tamales any good?" William asked. He was sitting at a picnic table with his back against it, his legs stretched out.

"Oh yes, they most certainly are," Emily said. She'd flown in the day before after settling the issues with the Alderman who'd been harassing her. Temporarily settled them, anyway. She'd barely let Sergio out of her sights since, and if they hadn't been at the rescheduled festival, she would have been glued to his side. Emily also settled her issue with Alex, telling her if she ever put Sergio in danger again she'd have to deal with her. Alex protested that Sergio was perfectly capable of taking care of himself and the two friends agreed to disagree.

Emily jumped up. "Best tamales I've ever had. Hey Jorge!" she shouted, then walked towards the banks of the river. The man paddled over. Emily slipped off her sandals, waded into the water to meet him, and handed him a wad of cash. She turned around with her arms full and a huge grin on her face. "Hey Alex, would you mind?"

Alex jumped up and ran over to get Emily's sandals. As she walked back to the table, she saw Sergio approaching, followed by Roger and a woman. Alex stopped. "Is that Officer Brooks?"

"In the flesh," Roger said, grinning.

"Call me Gabby," the woman said.

William turned around as Roger and Gabby sat at the picnic table, each of them holding a couple tasters of beer. Emily dumped her pile of tamales in the center and Sergio set down a few more tasters. "Compliments of Jody," he said. "This is her ESB."

They each picked up a glass. William raised his in a toast. "Here's to Raising the Beer!" The friends tapped their glasses and sipped, calling "Cheers!"

Alex looked around the park grounds. "Nice turnout, Sergio. Seems like there are even more people here than there were last week."

"There are," Roger confirmed. "People love drama."

"And beer," William said. "People love beer."

"And tamales. Don't forget the tamales," Emily said, her mouth full.

The group laughed. It had only been a couple of days since Detective Sato had arrested Candy for murdering her husband. She'd quickly switched from playing the victim to telling him and Detective Dunlap everything, beginning with how "the fool" had let her tie him up. That part of her earlier story had been true, but the drowning she'd done all on her own.

Alex thought back to Calliope's statement that drowning Mitchell in his own beer was too creative for Candy. Apparently it wasn't.

Detective Sato surprised everyone by apologizing to Sergio, telling him he knew he hadn't killed Mitchell, but by focusing on him, he and Dunlap had hoped to lull the real killer into a false sense of security. "Cold, man," Sergio had said. "Effective, but cold."

Alex watched Roger and Gabby. She still didn't trust him. She wasn't even sure she liked him, with his not-so-subtle misogyny and his, as Candy had put it, questionable moral character. Sergio didn't seem to have those doubts, and Alex hoped her friend wouldn't get burned. Alex faced Gabby. "So how did you end up at Roger's that night?"

She bobbed her head at Billy. "Billy called me. Told me you and William had cooked up some hairbrained scheme–"

"Which worked, by the way," William interrupted.

"—and requested some professional intervention, as a favor for another member of the force."

"So you didn't know Detective Sato was going to be there?" Alex asked.

"Of course I did. Who do you think called him?"

"I, for one, am glad you did. If I'd been tied up any longer, I might not have any hands or feet left." Sergio glared at Roger.

"Like I said, I had to sell it."

"Not that hard, man. Seriously." Sergio rubbed his wrists again in mock pain, then grinned and punched Roger in the shoulder.

"Thank you for calling in the pros, Billy," Emily said, then took another bite. "Oh, man, these are good."

"Someone's got to keep these two from getting themselves killed," Billy said, grabbing his own tamale. "I had no idea travel writing was such dangerous business."

William and Alex grinned at each other. "We just go where the story takes us, right, my friend?" William asked.

"Right," Alex said. She kept looking around the festival grounds, hoping to see a tall man with long black hair.

"If you're looking for Max, he's not here," Sergio said. "He's teaching Jackson how to take samples."

Alex's face fell, ever so slightly. "That's fine. I was hoping to say goodbye. To both of them, I mean."

"I thought you were leaving on Monday?" William asked.

Alex shook her head. "I am, but I promised Calliope we'd hang out tomorrow."

Sergio eyed her. "Oh?"

Alex smiled softly at him, but didn't say anything. The young woman had approached her shyly the night before, saying she loved brewing and was grateful to Sergio, but she wanted to see more of the world and thought she might be ready to think about doing something else with her life. Alex told her she'd be delighted to fill her in on what it was like to be a travel writer, both the good and the bad. Alex guessed Calliope needed someone to talk to, for career advice and other reasons, and she was glad to be that person.

"You guys started the party without me? Not fair. Not fair at all." A man that Alex had only seen at the police station reached the picnic table, holding a taster. He sat on the edge of the bench next to Alex, flipping his sandy blonde hair and extending his hand. "I don't believe we've met formally. I'm Ethan."

Alex took his hand. A jolt of electricity shot up her arm, and she tilted her head, smiling with her eyes. "Hi Ethan. I'm Alex." She noticed his glass was empty, then drained hers. "Looks like you need another drink, and so do I. Would you like to join me?"

He grinned. "I'd love to."

I hope you enjoyed spending time with Alex, William, and the entire cast. Follow their next adventures in *Chaos in the Canyon*. When a travel conference in Montana turns deadly, Alex finds herself racing against time to clear her best friend's name. With a killer on the loose and a priceless artifact at stake, Alex's knack for uncovering the truth will be put to the ultimate test. Pack your bags and join Alex for a Montana mystery that's as vast and unpredictable as Big Sky Country itself. thelocaltourist.com/chaos

BONUS: save 20% on Alex Paige's adventures at theresas books.com! Use code RUIN20.

For even more Alex, find out how her travel writing career began—with a crime, of course! She's barely off the plane for her first research trip when she encounters the police. Will the Sonoran Desert, and her new career, prove too hot for her to handle? Visit thelocaltourist.com/go/stolen/ to get your free short story, *Stolen on the Salt River*.

Recipe
Short Ribs, Bacon, and Beer Chili

If you think Sergio's chili sounded amazing, you'd be right. It's rich and has some serious depth to it (unlike Greg Mitchell). Wondering what that special flavor was? Check the last ingredient.

Ingredients

- 2 lbs boneless beef short ribs, cut into small pieces

- 1/2 lb thick-cut bacon, chopped

- 1 large onion, chopped

- 1 red bell pepper, diced

- 4 cloves garlic, minced

- 1 can (15 oz) kidney beans, drained and rinsed

- 1 can (15 oz) black beans, drained and rinsed

- 2 cans (15 oz each) fire-roasted diced tomatoes

- 1 cup dark beer (like stout or porter)

- 1 cup strong brewed coffee

- 2 cups beef broth

- 3 tbsp chili powder

- 1 tbsp ground cumin

- 1 tsp smoked paprika

- 1/2 tsp cayenne pepper (adjust to taste)

- Salt and black pepper to taste

- 2 tbsp tomato paste

- Honey (optional)

- 2 oz dark chocolate (70% cocoa)

Instructions

1. Cook bacon in a large pot until crispy; remove and set aside.

2. Brown short ribs in bacon fat; remove and set aside.

3. Sauté onion, bell pepper, and garlic in the same pot.

4. Add back the bacon, short ribs, beans, tomatoes, tomato paste, beer, coffee, and beef broth.

5. Stir in spices and simmer for at least 2 hours.

6. Before serving, stir in dark chocolate until melted. Add honey to taste.

7. Adjust seasoning and serve with shredded cheese, lime crema, cilantro, diced red onions, sliced jalapenos, or whatever else you like on your chili.

Author Note

In the summer of 2022, I took a solo road trip. After teaching a writing workshop in Billings, Montana, I headed west. I didn't know where I was going to camp for the night, but I envisioned an evergreen-shaded site overlooking a rocky creek.

I found it.

I also found a family of four. They were spread out in the site next to me. These sites were huge, so I couldn't even eavesdrop. However, they realized I was by myself and invited me to join them for a drink. I said yes, and during our conversation I learned he was a Riverkeeper.

I'd never heard of such a thing, but the idea captured me. I found out he monitored the French Broad River in Western North Carolina, where my parents live. Immediately, I knew I'd write about him some day; I just didn't know in what form.

Max's career is inspired by this stranger I met in the mountains of Montana. His temper is not.

Although this book is set in the Asheville area, the only real places mentioned are the French Broad River and the Biltmore, in Max's derisive comment. The rest is inspired by that beautiful area. There are creeks everywhere (and waterfalls, too). There's a large city park along the French Broad that inspired the setting for the festival. The CCC did set up camps in the Smoky Mountains while building the Blue Ridge Parkway, but Sergio's setting for Layers came out of my head.

In some ways, I wish I'd been able to include more of Asheville itself. It's an artistic, vibrant city. But, I go where the story leads, and the story wanted to focus on the characters more than the place.

The brewery scene in Asheville is phenomenal. I spent a couple weeks there cat- and house-sitting for my parents and visited thirty-one breweries in twelve days. Jody and her Basil Bitter were inspired by Whaley Farms Brewing. Fonta Flora's field of marigolds inspired Calliope's signature beer. That hazy IPA that Alex and Emily loved? It's reminiscent of a beer I tried at Burial.

I'm also familiar with the camaraderie that exists within the brewing community. Pre-pandemic, I'd hosted seventeen AlphaBeer events, where attendees would try a beer from every letter of the alphabet, and guest brewers joined us to talk about their craft.

Will I revisit Asheville in another book and show more of its wonders? Maybe. But not yet. Until then, I hope you enjoyed this homage to one of the most beautiful areas of the country.

Acknowledgments

With four Alex Paige books under my belt, you'd think it would get easier. But as I've heard from countless other authors, it doesn't.

Is it fun? Oh, yes. Writing these books gives me pure joy. Is it easy?

Sort of.

There are days the words flow. Other days they're like stubborn teenagers, refusing to cooperate with anything I want to do. Often, the first words I type are, "I have no idea what happens next." Then I close my eyes, re-read the last few paragraphs, and trust.

Eventually, a book emerges.

Then comes the hard part of editing, and editing, and editing. Making sure everything makes sense. The hard part of putting this creation into someone else's hands and inviting them to punch holes in it, rip it apart, point out anything and everything I did wrong.

(Makes you want to write a book, doesn't it?)

But, they also laugh and tell me to hurry up because they want to know what happens next. To Heidi Kohz, Mom, and Dad, thank you. Thank you for not holding back when something needs fixed or you find a cliche or I don't go into enough detail or whatever. You make my work so much better, so much stronger.

Tatiana, I will forever and always thank you because I will forever and always hear your voice in my head while I'm writing, and especially when I'm editing. I'm a cleaner and more captivating writer (your lovely words) because of you.

To my faithful and supportive readers: Larry and Carol Pratt, Karen Gill, Shelly Harms, Henri Goudsmit, and many others — thank you for pre-ordering. Knowing you're waiting spurs me on.

I'd also like to thank the many attendees of the Travel and Adventure Shows in Chicago, Denver, and Los Angeles who ordered the whole Alex Paige series, even though you knew nothing about it. I'm honored you've taken a chance on this new-to-you author, and am looking forward to your feedback.

And to Jim. Your belief, support, and love help me get through the tough days, the days of self-doubt, the struggles of trying to meet my own impossible standards. You lift me up and put up with my disconcerting focus on dead bodies and ways to kill someone. Thank you, my love.

And thank you to everyone who meets Alex Paige and her collection of opinionated friends. I'm excited to show you where she ends up next!

Also By Theresa L. Carter

As Theresa L. Carter

Alex Paige Books 1-5
Get the first five Alex Paige adventures!
Peril on the Peninsula
Revenge in the Rockies
Betrayed at the Beach
Ruin on the River
Chaos in the Canyon
Menace at the Marina

As Theresa L. Goodrich

Two Lane Gems, Vol. 1
Turkeys are Jerks and Other Observations from an American Road Trip
Two Lane Gems, Vol. 2
Bison are Giant and Other Observations from an American Road Trip
Living Landmarks of Chicago
Planning Your Perfect Road Trip

Show Me Shipshewana
A Guide to Indiana Amish Country
Discover Geary County, Kansas
Nature, History, and Hometown Hospitality in the Sunflower State

Publisher / Contributor

Midwest Road Trip Adventures, 2nd Edition
Midwest State Park Adventures

About Theresa L. Carter

Theresa's one of those voracious readers who grew up with her nose in a book and the desire to write her own. That took some time, as she spent years telling people where to go as a full-time travel writer before making it happen when she was 47 (because you're never too old to start). That book, *Turkeys are Jerks and Other Observations from an American Road Trip*, lit a long-dormant fire, and she's continued to write and publish travel books at a rapid pace ever since. She still wanted to write novels, though, and after a breast cancer gut punch, decided at age 51 not to wait any more. Alex Paige sprung out of her head, Athena-like, and hasn't left her alone since.

When Theresa's not telling people where to go or being told by Alex and friends what to write, she's reading (of course), learning, cooking, figuring out how to spend as much time outside as possible, or annoying her husband.

And sometimes, all of the above.

You can find Theresa on social media @theresastoryteller and at theresasbooks.com